P9-CEY-127

This book is in aid of Kids Company, the charity founded by Camila Batmanghelidjh in 1996 to provide practical, emotional and educational support to vulnerable inner-city children and young people. Find out more at **www.kidsco.org.uk**.

All the authors who have generously donated their stories were shortlisted for the first Queen of Teen awards. The world's most glamorous book prize returns in 2010 – for news about this year's shortlist and all the latest gossip from Queen of Teen HQ, visit **www.queenofteen.co.uk**.

In aid of

KIDS
COMPANY

Queen of Teen

FABULOUS STORIES
FROM TOP TEEN AUTHORS

Meg Cabot • Cathy Cassidy • Lisa Clark
Cathy Hopkins • Sarra Manning • Karen McCombie
Joanna Nadin • Louise Rennison • Jacqueline Wilson

Piccadilly Press • London

STATE LIBRARY OF WESTERN AUSTRALIA

First published in Great Britain in 2010
by Piccadilly Press Ltd,
5 Castle Road, London NW1 8PR
www.piccadillypress.co.uk

Text copyright
Sink or Swim © Cathy Cassidy 2010
Problems © Jacqueline Wilson 2010
Big Red Bottomosity © Louise Rennison 2003 and 2010
This story is adapted from an episode first published in its entirety
by HarperCollins Children's Books US in Knocked Out By My
Nunga-Nungas. Parts of the story were first published in the UK by
Piccadilly Press under the same title, which is now published by
HarperCollins Children's Books, a division of
HarperCollinsPublishers Ltd, 77 – 85 Fulham Palace Road,
Hammersmith, London N6 8JB.
Mum Never Did Learn To Knock © Cathy Hopkins 2010
Digger Number 5 © Meg Cabot 2010
B.L.D. © Karen McCombie 2010
How To Be A Star © Lisa Clark 2010
A Life Less Ordinary © Joanna Nadin 2010
Some Girls Are Bigger Than Others © Sarra Manning 2010
All rights reserved. No part of this publication may be reproduced,
stored in a retrieval system, or transmitted
in any form or by any means electronic, mechanical,
photocopying, recording or otherwise, without the
prior permission of the copyright owner.

The rights of Cathy Cassidy, Jacqueline Wilson,
Louise Rennison, Cathy Hopkins, Meg Cabot,
Karen McCombie, Lisa Clark, Joanna Nadin
and Sarra Manning to be identified as Authors of this
work has been asserted by them in accordance with the
Copyright, Designs and Patents Act 1988

A catalogue record for this book is available
from the British Library

ISBN: 978 1 84812 072 3 (paperback)
978 1 84812 108 9 (bookclub hardback)

1 3 5 7 9 10 8 6 4 2

Printed and bound in the UK by J F Print Ltd., Sparkford
Cover design: Simon Davis
Cover illustration: Sue Hellard

Contents

Foreword
by Camila
Batmanghelidjh

Teenagers are often profoundly misrepresented in the media. Journalistic laziness results in the average teenager being stereotyped. Either they're spotty, clueless and drunk, buried in the rubble of unwashed dishes in their bedrooms, or they're menacingly hidden in their hoods, waiting to attack.

So you can imagine our delight at Kids Company when such wonderful writers decided to contribute and help us raise money for the incredible teenagers we work with. The world should be celebrating its young people. So many are inspirational, enthusiastic and generous, always coming up with questions and innovations which propel humanity towards greater achievement. Teenagers pull us all up towards life. Even those who are living with profound poverty and surviving abuse show astounding levels of courage. They forgive their parents when harm has been caused, defend their siblings and remain hopeful when hopelessness would have been easier.

Kids Company provides wrap-around care for some 14,000 vulnerable children and teenagers. Ninety-five per cent of those seeking help have heard about us at street level and are asking for help directly, without an adult to pay for the services we provide. Therefore, as a charity, we are hugely reliant on public donations to enable us to remain a sanctuary for abused children. Your donation through buying this book will make a big difference in a young person's life. They will know someone cares. In being less lonely, they can cope better with the pain of being hurt.

So thank you to all those brilliant writers who have donated their stories, and to you, the reader, for making *Queen of Teen* your choice.

With love,

Camila
Chief Executive
Kids Company

Cathy Cassidy
Sink or Swim

'You?' Courtney says scornfully. 'There must be some mistake, some kind of mix-up. Why would they choose *you*?'

I blink, pink-cheeked, and tilt my chin up, bravely. 'I don't know,' I say. 'But they did.'

We are standing at the bus stop after school, waiting for the 73a. I have stood at this exact same bus stop with Courtney Taylor every school day for the last two and a half years, and she has never spoken to me before. I am not sure if she actually knew I was alive, until today.

Courtney frowns at the letter in her hand and then looks at me, narrowing her eyes. 'It doesn't make sense,' she huffs, flicking back her long, blond hair. 'The teachers were supposed to match us all up with our perfect work experience placement . . . and they go and pick *you* to work with Bella Marlow. It doesn't seem fair!'

'Hey,' my best friend Kate chips in, loyally. 'Of course it's fair! Bella Marlow picked Millie . . . she's the best person for the job.'

You cannot reason with Courtney Taylor, though. She is the coolest girl in Year Nine, the self-styled star of Castleford Academy. She is smart, she is pretty, she has enough confidence to last her a lifetime. When I stand next to Courtney, I'm not just in her shadow, I am practically invisible.

'I was the obvious choice,' Courtney is scowling. 'Bella Marlow is a legend. She was one of Britain's top models, until a decade ago, and now she's probably the best fashion photographer of her generation . . . her pictures are in all the glossy mags. And I am going to be a model, so I would be the best person for the placement, right?'

'Apparently not,' Kate says. 'Right, Millie?'

'Erm . . .'

A whole bunch of us applied for a work experience placement with Bella Marlow. A week helping out in her studio was always going to be a million times better than the usual week of shelf-stacking in a local supermarket or whatever other delights the school could come up with. The problem was, Bella only wanted one work experience pupil.

I never imagined in a million years she'd pick me.

'I don't know if you understand . . . um, Millie, is it?'
Courtney snaps. 'This could have been my big break! And now
that chance is going to be wasted . . . on you. That sucks.'

Kate raises an eyebrow. She has landed her own dream
work experience placement, at a top hairdresser's in town,
and I think a little bit of her is enjoying Courtney's stroppy
attitude. It's not often that we get to see the Year Nine starlet
throw a tantrum.

'What's up, Courtney?' Kate asks, sweetly. 'Not jealous, are
you?'

Courtney examines her pale pink fingernails. 'Jealous?' she
snarls. 'Not a chance. Good luck with your placement, Millie
. . . I have a feeling you'll need it!'

The bus arrives and Courtney elbows her way to the front
and gets on, blond hair swishing.

'I don't like Courtney Taylor,' I say. 'She has a nasty streak . . .'

'About a mile wide,' Kate agrees. 'I don't think she is model
material, unless maybe it was an advert for sour grapes.'

Kate and I find a seat together near the back.

'Want to know what Courtney's placement is?' Kate grins.
'She's going to be working in a factory that makes thermal
underwear. You know, long-johns and woolly vests and big
knickers that come down to your knees . . . No wonder she's
mad at you!'

I picture Courtney Taylor packing thermal knickers and
polo-necked vests into boxes, and I have to smile.

'She might be right, though,' I confess to Kate. 'What if I

am out of my depth at Bella Marlow's studio? What if I can't cope?'

Kate rolls her eyes. 'You'll cope,' she tells me, firmly. 'You work about a million times harder than Courtney Taylor, and you are not a quitter. And you are great with a camera, Millie – that's why they picked you! They read your application letter and they recognised someone who really loves photography.'

'I know, but . . .'

'No buts,' Kate insists. 'You are the best person for that placement, end of story. If you were Bella Marlow, who would you pick? A talented young photography student or a would-be model who just wanted to grab a chance to be in the limelight? Think about it!'

I frown. 'But . . . Kate, it's *fashion* photography,' I sigh. 'That's scary. It's a different world. What if I don't fit in?'

Thing is, it is not just Courtney Taylor who thinks I am the invisible girl. I am plain, I am shy, I am ordinary. My eyes are the colour of muddy puddles, my hair is a mousey brown and wavy and shoulder-length. I do not have the knack of making a navy blue school uniform into a fashion statement.

There is nothing about me that stands out from the crowd. I am a wallpaper girl – I blend into the background.

'Hey,' Kate says. 'You'll be fine!'

I look at Kate, blinking at me from beneath a scene-girl fringe, her eyes rimmed with smoky eyeliner, and I look at Courtney, chatting to a gaggle of Year Ten boys a few seats down from us, her hair perfectly cut and layered and streaked, and straightened to within an inch of its life.

They have style – and confidence.

I don't.

'You have to believe in yourself,' Kate says, echoing my thoughts. 'It's all about self-esteem. You're as good as Courtney Taylor, any day – better, honest! You're pretty and clever and kind and talented . . .'

Well, Kate would say that, I guess. She's my best friend. Loyalty is part of her job-description.

'You're cool, Millie,' Kate says. 'Believe it! And trust me, Bella Marlow won't care one bit whether you are wearing Converse and jeans or a slinky dress with Jimmy Choos. It's a work placement, not a fashion parade!'

'But . . . what if I'm out of my depth?'

Kate laughs. 'Sometimes, you have to risk being out of your depth,' she says. 'What's the worst that can happen? You either sink or you swim. You can't stay in the shallows all your life.'

'Do I get armbands?' I ask with a grin, and Kate jabs me in the ribs, laughing.

'You won't need them,' she tells me. 'Promise!'

I look in the mirror and a pale, big-eyed girl stares back at me. She has a little green eyeliner smudged around her eyes, a spotted headband holding back her wavy hair. She is wearing a simple blue T-shirt, skinny jeans, Rocket Dog pumps bought specially for the occasion. She looks scared.

If she was my friend, I'd tell her to relax, smile, enjoy the adventure, but I'm not sure if she'd listen. She's remembering the things Courtney Taylor said, mean things, spiteful things. Her fingers shake as she applies pink lip-gloss, tries for a smile.

'Sink or swim,' I tell her, and the girl in the mirror lifts her head and grins.

I think maybe she has had enough of hanging around in the shallows, enough of being a wallpaper girl.

At Bella Marlow's studio, I ring the bell for ages and then a boy with a dipping sky-blue fringe sticks his head out of an upstairs window and asks if I am the new work experience girl. Then he throws down two twenty-pound notes and asks me to run over to Starbucks for lattes – three skinny, one with soya, one chai, a mint tea and a bunch of muffins. 'Oh,' he adds, 'and whatever you want, too!'

I catch the money before it drifts into the gutter, my heart thumping. This is not what I had in mind, but I don't want to mess up on my first day. I run to Starbucks, and ten minutes later I am back at the studio, clutching a cardboard box full of lattes and muffins.

The blue-fringe boy opens the door and takes the cardboard box, checking through the contents. 'Perfect!' he says. 'That's a first, for a work experience kid. Come in . . . I'm Martin, Bella's assistant . . .'

A tall, striking woman in her thirties appears behind Martin.

'And I'm Bella. Good to meet you, Millie!'

Bella Marlow still has the long auburn curls and startling blue-green eyes that made her such a famous face in her modelling days, but there is nothing starry about her. She is simply dressed in combats and a plain white T-shirt, her hair tied back and her face free of make-up.

'I hope you'll enjoy your week with us,' she says, ushering me inside as Martin runs up a flight of stairs with the coffee supplies. 'I was very impressed with your letter... you sounded very different from the usual work experience kids we get. You take your own photos, right? I loved the prints you sent in with your application. They really had something . . . you have a talent.'

'Oh . . . thank you!' I stammer. 'I can't believe you chose me. You must have had so many fantastic applicants...'

Bella frowns. 'I did,' she says, 'and I chose you, because you were the best.'

My cheeks flush pink.

'I have to tell you, though, photography is a tough business,' she continues. 'Talent isn't always enough. You have to work hard.'

'I can work hard,' I say.

'I think you can,' Bella smiles. 'But more than that, you have to be determined. You have to get out there and make your mark. You cannot be shy or retiring, and you cannot hide away in the background. You have to believe in yourself.'

I blink. 'That's not always easy,' I say in a small voice, and Bella laughs.

'No, it's not easy, but it's true all the same,' she says. 'You remind me of me, back when I was your age, Millie. A little shy, a little unsure. But, honey, you're as good as anyone! Believe it!'

'I . . . OK!'

'You won't have time to hide away in the background, here,' Bella says. 'This is a crazy week for us – publicity shots, fashion shots, a magazine spread . . . we'll barely have time to stop and draw breath. We'll work you hard, I warn you, Millie, but I think you'll enjoy it.'

'I will!' I grin.

Bella gives me a quick tour of the studios. There's a dressing room, where a model is sipping mint tea through a straw while a make-up artist paints her eyelids with glittery green shadow and a stylist is ironing a bundle of satin dresses in jewel-bright colours; upstairs, there is the studio proper, where Martin, the blue-fringe boy, is struggling with a roll of backdrop paper and a whole forest of blazing lights.

'Can you grab this?' Martin asks, and I drop my bag and stretch up to hold the backdrop while he adjusts the lighting.

'I'll leave you to it,' Bella says, checking her watch. 'Martin'll keep you busy, show you the ropes. We're shooting in five minutes, OK? Chin up, Millie! It's in at the deep end, I'm afraid!'

'Sink or swim,' I say.

'You got it,' Bella grins, 'but I think you'll swim. I'm counting on it, Millie.'

I have never worked so hard in my whole, entire life. I am the studio dogsbody.

Sometimes I am adjusting the lights and fixing up the tripods, sometimes I am holding a silver reflector right under the face of an up-and-coming model to make her look more radiant. Those things are pretty good. Sometimes, though, I am brushing the studio floor or polishing shoes or balancing on a stepladder, hanging muslin drapes across the set. I have become an expert at ironing dresses and I have made so many trips to Starbucks the assistants know me by name.

There's even one especially crazy day when one of the models doesn't turn up for a teen-mag fashion shoot, and Bella says we don't have time to wait for the agency to send a replacement, so the stylist does my make-up and fixes me up with a sugar-pink wig to match the other model. We head out to one of the big London parks and shoot all afternoon until the light fades, me and the other model wearing pastel-coloured prom dresses and feeding the ducks and the swans.

When I see the photos on Bella's laptop, I don't even recognise myself. I think of Courtney Taylor and her dreams of being a model . . . what would she say if she could see this? She might see it, one day, and still she'd never guess.

That makes me smile.

I begin dreaming of pink hair and pretty prom dresses, and I wonder if Bella is a kind of fairy godmother, because when she is around I forget to be shy.

I don't have time to be, anyhow.

I've started to realise that blue fringes and designer jeans are nothing to be scared of. People are just people, whatever they look like, whatever they say, whatever their job description might be. They can be nice or nasty or clever or kind, and that's what matters in the end.

'Why the blue fringe?' I ask Martin one day, as we sift glittery fake snow over a set draped with white velvet, ready for a Christmas shoot. 'I've been wondering.'

Martin does not strike me as a blue-fringe kind of a boy. He works so hard it's a miracle he has time to comb his hair, let alone dye it the colour of the sky in summer, but I am learning not to judge a book by its cover.

'Thinking of going pink, like in the fashion shoot?' he teases.

'No way!' I protest. 'I'd never dare.'

'Rubbish,' he says. 'You can do whatever you want to do. Do you really want to know why I went blue?'

'I really do.'

'It makes a statement.' Martin shrugs. 'People notice it, and they make their own assumptions. That I am confident, that I am arty, that I am cool. That's fine. It means I can get on with my job and forget about trying to impress people.' Suddenly he looks straight at me. 'I didn't think I could fit into this world, to start with. D'you want to know what my nickname was at school?'

'What?'

'Mouse,' he says.

I sit on the wall with Kate, huddled into my coat, a floppy beanie hat pulled low on my head, waiting for the 73a bus to school.

'That,' says Kate, 'was the best week of my life, I swear.'

'Me, too,' I say. 'It was awesome. I'll never forget it.'

'No wonder,' Kate grins. 'You're a super-model, now, right? With trendy blue-fringed friends and the offer of a summer holiday job with Bella Marlow. Courtney will be green with envy.'

'I wonder how she got on at the knicker factory?' I ask.

'Here she is,' Kate says. 'I think we are about to find out . . .'

Courtney heads straight for us, head held high. 'Oh. My. God,' she breathes, flicking her perfect hair. 'I have had the most amazing week, you just would not believe . . .'

'Oh?' I say. 'What was it like?'

'Well, of course, it was an actual fashion house,' Courtney beams. 'Specialising in exclusive . . . erm . . . lingerie. For the more . . . er . . . mature client. So for someone aiming for a career in the fashion industry, it couldn't have been more perfect. I was involved with every stage of the process, from design to production to packing . . .'

'Packing boxes,' Kate whispers. 'Nice.'

'And – well, let's just say, who needs Bella Marlow?' Courtney goes on. 'I mean, everyone says her work is past its best. Not exactly cutting edge.'

I bite my lip.

'Well, anyway, I am glad I didn't waste my work placement there,' Courtney says, 'because I actually got the modelling break I was looking for. I'm going to be famous!'

'Really?' I ask. I am pleased for Courtney, because I know what it's like to want something badly. I want to be a photographer – I want that more than ever, now, after my week with Bella Marlow. And I want to move out from the shallows, too. I want to be brave, make my mark, take risks. Sink or swim.

'Yes, really,' Courtney smirks. 'While I was there, the company were shooting their new catalogue. And, obviously, they had professional models for it, but they recognised my potential and I was allowed to appear in some of the shots. My big break!'

'Courtney!' I exclaim. 'That's fantastic! I'm so happy for you!'

'Well, you know,' she says. 'Talent shines through.'

'I expect it does,' Kate smiles. 'Do you have the shots?'

Courtney looks shifty. 'I do,' she admits. 'I mean, it'll be a while before the catalogue is printed up, of course, but they gave me a couple of prints . . . it might not be easy for you to see just how they'll look . . .'

'We'll use our imagination,' Kate says.

Courtney brings a gold-edged folder out of her bag and opens it carefully, fanning out the prints inside. I catch a glimpse of a shapely ankle encased in a tartan slipper. Beside me, Kate stifles a laugh, trying to disguise it as a sneeze.

'This is . . . you?' I ask.

'Yes,' Courtney says briskly, not quite meeting our eyes. 'This is me. The start of my modelling career.' She puts the folder away and gives Kate and I a pitying glance.

'So . . . how did your placements go?' she asks. 'I expect you were overlooked, really, Millie, at Bella Marlow's studio? Such a waste.'

'Oh, you know,' I shrug. 'It was OK.'

'How about you, Kate?' Courtney asks.

'Oh, the usual,' Kate says. 'Shampooing old ladies, sweeping up hair clippings, helping with perms and tints . . . I did get to help dye a friend's hair Barbie pink, though, on the last day. That was cool.'

'A friend?' Courtney echoes. 'Yeah, right. By the way, Millie, I like your hat. It's nice to see you making a bit of an effort for a change.'

I pull a face. 'I'm not so sure about the hat,' I confess. 'I'm not really into this whole fashion thing . . .'

Courtney smiles, the kind of smile a crocodile gives to a little fish before swallowing it whole. 'Some people are just not cut out to turn heads, Millie,' she says. 'Don't worry. Just be yourself – nobody will mind.'

'I guess you're right,' I say. I pull off the hat and grin at

15

Courtney through a fall of bright, Barbie-pink hair, and watch her eyes open wide and her jaw drop towards the pavement.

The wallpaper girl has vanished, never to be seen again. I am not invisible any more.

The 73a draws up and Kate and I get on, leaving Courtney to scramble after us.

'Sink or swim,' Kate whispers, but we both know there's nothing to be scared of any more.

We're swimming, and the tide is with us . . . and it feels great.

Jacqueline Wilson
Problems

Miss Drummond drones on and on about these awful maths problems. I can't understand maths even if I concentrate until steam comes out of my ears. Besides, I've got other things on my mind. I doodle on the back of my maths book, writing my name in all sorts of fancy ways and surrounding each posh squiggly signature with elaborately entwined flowers. Then I write down Damian Chatham. He's this boy I like in our class. He's not my boyfriend. I wish! Damian's not the most good-looking boy and he's not the cleverest and he's not the best at sports – but he's funny and kind and I like him lots, though I'm too shy to let on to anyone, apart from my friend Lucy.

I don't know if Damian likes me or not. He said he liked my long hair once. And another time when I dropped the ball in rounders and everyone groaned, he said quietly, 'Don't worry, Nicola.' But that doesn't really mean anything. He's nice to everyone. He's nice to my friend Lucy. She's nuts about him too.

There's a little poke in my back. I turn around. Lucy passes me a note, keeping a wary eye on Miss Drummond. I have a peek under my desk.

Dear Nicola – Isn't this BORING!!! Do you have a clue what she's on about? Jenny and Mags and I are going down the Rec near my house after school. Want to come? Love Lucy

P.S. Damian and his mates often hang out there.

I read Lucy's note. I read it again. I read the last line over and over. I want to go down to the Rec with Lucy and Jenny and Mags – and maybe Damian! – soooo much. But I can't.

Dear Lucy – I write – Sorry, I can't make it after school. Don't you dare get off with Damian yourself! I haven't got a clue about the maths problems either. Old Drummond could be talking in some obscure Tuareg dialect for all I know –

Lucy never gets my note because Miss Drummond stops her long involved mathematical discourse and sees me scribbling. She asks me what I'm writing. I say, 'Nothing, Miss Drummond.' She sighs, beckons and holds out her hand. I have to give her the note. She raises her eyebrows at the Old Drummond Tuareg bit. I hold my breath.

I'm terrified she'll give me a detention. I have to get back home for Mum. They know a bit about her at school, but they don't know how bad things are now. They still think Dad's around anyway. We can't tell them in case they have to report it.

It's almost a relief when Miss Drummond sets me extra maths homework instead. I won't be able to do it, of course. I'll have to suck up to Clever Clogs Chrissie and bribe her with the Kit Kat from my packed lunch to see if she'll do the maths problems for me.

'Sorry you got caught, Nicks,' says Lucy, when the bell goes. 'You coming to the Rec, then?'

'I can't, Lucy.'

'You *can*. Look, I tell you, I heard Damian chatting to Jack and Liam and Little Pete. They're planning to play footie there.'

'You know I have to do the shopping for my mum.'

'Yeah but you could do that after.'

'I can't be late for her.'

Lucy sighs. She knows about my mum and me. I've sworn her to secrecy. But she doesn't understand. 'You've got to have some life of your *own*, Nicola,' she says. Like it's a life choice I can make.

Lucy's my best friend, but sometimes I feel like we're poles apart. She's at the North Pole spinning under the stars with Jenny and Mags and Jack and Liam and Little Pete and my Damian – and I'm down at the South Pole all by myself, unable to get hold of my own life.

I rush off without even saying goodbye properly. I don't want Lucy to see I've got tears in my eyes. I blink furiously and hurry down to Tesco's and buy all the food and stuff. Then I have to go to Boots and stand at the counter with these big packs of incontinence pads. I should be used to it by now but I still go bright red, scared that people will think they're for *me*, though I know no one can help being incontinent and it's nothing to be ashamed of.

I peer just for a moment in Primark but I haven't got time for a proper look and there's no point anyway. We haven't got any spare cash.

Then I lumber everything home. There's no bus that goes near our flats and taxis are out of the question. My arms ache and I feel hot and tired and fed up. I can't help thinking about Lucy and the girls down at the Rec, sitting on the swings, giggling away, watching Damian and the others kicking a football about. Then the ball gets kicked near them, Lucy catches it, Damian comes running over, they have a little laugh together, Lucy tosses her lovely shiny hair out of her eyes, Damian stares at her, smiles . . .

It's as if it's actually happening in front of me. It's not *fair*.

But it's stupid getting worked up about it. 'Stupid, stupid, stupid,' I hiss to myself as I go into our estate. I keep my eyes down and just nod quickly whenever anyone says hello. We can't have anyone getting too friendly and coming round. If they saw how bad mum is now, they'd maybe start interfering.

I have to trail up three flights of stairs because the lifts are broken again. Just as well we don't live right up on the fifteenth floor. Still, I don't suppose it makes much difference to Mum.

I stop in front of our door. I wipe my eyes. I breathe deeply. I stretch my lips into a great big smile. Then I let myself in.

'Cooee, Mum,' I go, as I always do.

There's a little pause, my heart thumps – but then, faintly, 'Cooee, Nicky,' comes from the living room.

I dump the shopping in the hall and go and see her. She's got her bag open and a tissue in her hand. Maybe she was having a little weep herself? Her eyes look red. But she's got her own smile firmly fixed in place.

'Hi there, my best girl,' she says.

'Wotcha, my best Mum,' I say. 'Cup of tea?'

'Yes, please,' she says, but her smile slips. 'Oh Nicky, if only I could have a cup of tea waiting for *you*, like a proper mum.'

'Oh, so you're an *improper* mum?' I say quickly, taking her lunchtime tray. She's tipped her cup over but she's started using one of those with a lid and a spout so it didn't spill. She's got sandwich crumbs all down her front though. She sees me looking and tries to brush them away but her hands are so feeble nowadays they're not much use. She tries so hard to keep herself nice but on a bad day she can't even brush her hair or do her own make-up. Some days she doesn't feel like it anyway. She just says 'What's the point?' and sits and stares into space. Those are the scariest days.

My mum's got this progressive illness. It means she can't get better. She can only get worse. She can't manage more than a couple of steps now. She can't lift anything with her hands. She can't get to the loo in time. She can't even bath herself now.

Mum hasn't always been like this. She used to be fit and healthy and strong. Stronger than most mums. I remember one day when I was little and we were on holiday at the seaside. Mum and I were paddling together, holding hands, jumping the waves – but then a big wave came and I slipped and went under. I got scared but Mum scooped me up and whirled me round and round so that my toes skimmed the water and it was just like I was flying. We ran races along the sand later to get warm, and Mum always beat me. She could even beat my dad.

He cleared off last year. He was OK when Mum was first diagnosed. She was just a bit clumsy and fell over every now and then. Dad helped her and said he was sure she'd get better in time. But she didn't get better, she gradually got worse. Dad cried the first time she had to use a wheelchair. He said it made him feel so bad. How did he think it made Mum feel?

Dad got more and more depressed and started staying out late. He said it was because he couldn't bear to watch Mum suffer. But he'd started seeing this woman at his work. He lives with her now. He still sends us money – well, most of the time. But he hardly ever comes to see us. Still, we manage fine without him.

Well, we did. But it's getting harder and harder now. Mum's getting worse. She won't see the doctor anymore. She says there's no point because he can't cure her. Mum won't see anyone in case they tell on us. If people find out that dad's gone for good and I'm the only one looking after Mum, then they might split us up. Mum would end up in a home and I'd end up in care.

We couldn't bear that. We've got to stay together no matter what. So it's like I've taken over. I'm like the mum and she's like my little baby. I do everything for her. I don't *want* to. I get fed up lots of times. But what else can I do?

I know that one day Mum will get so bad she won't be able to be left alone. I don't know what I'm going to do then. I've thought about dashing home at lunchtime, bunking off school altogether – but then they'd investigate.

It's like one of Miss Drummond's maths problems. I can't seem to come up with any answer. And sometimes when Lucy goes on and on about her life being so unfair because her mum won't buy her this new leather jacket or her dad won't let her go to a disco, I just stare at her and think, if only I had *your* problems, Lucy. But I don't go on at her. Lucy's my friend. Even if she does get to go off with Damian.

I think about them as I make Mum's tea and sort her out. I think about them as Mum and I watch telly while we eat. I think about them as I do the dishes and put the sheets in the washing machine and start on yesterday's ironing.

Then the phone rings.

It'll be Lucy. All set to show off. Telling me about her and Damian.

'Nicky? It won't be for me,' Mum calls.

'Oh I'm busy, Mum,' I yell from the kitchen. 'It doesn't matter. Just let it ring.'

It rings and rings. I hear Mum grunt as she drags herself sideways, reaching out for it with one shaky hand.

'Don't, Mum!' I shout – but she's already answering.

'Nicky?' Mum calls. 'Someone to speak to you.'

I sigh. I close my eyes. I practise saying, 'Good for you, Lucy. Sure, it's cool with me. I hope you and Damian are very happy.'

But it's not Lucy. When I trudge into the living room, Mum mouths at me, 'It's a boy!' She grins at my shocked face.

My hands are shaking as I snatch up the phone.

'Hi, Nicola. It's me, Damian.'

I swallow. I say 'hi' back in such a silly squeak he doesn't hear me.

'Nicola?'

'Hello, Damian.'

'I've just been at the Rec with my mates.'

'Oh. Yeah?'

'And Lucy and them were there too.'

Oh no, *he's* going to tell me that they've made friends.

'Right,' I say tensely.

'I hoped you might be there too.'

'Oh. No. I – I had things to do.'

'Yes, Lucy said. I asked her for your phone number. I hope that's all right?'

'Mmm.' My heart is beating so fast I'm sure he can hear it.

'Lucy said your Mum's not well and you have to do the shopping and that?'

'Yes.'

'Well, maybe – maybe I could help you with the shopping sometimes?'

'With your mates?'

'No! Just you and me. I could help you carry the bags. If you'd like?'

'Oh. Well.' Thank goodness I've just stocked up at Boots! But I suppose it wouldn't matter if he came round Tesco's with me. In fact, it would be wonderful.

Mum is looking at me, nodding determinedly. 'Say YES!' she mouths.

'Okay then. Yes. If you're sure you wouldn't mind.'

'I'd like to. Okay? Well, see you at school tomorrow and we'll maybe go shopping after.'

'Yes. Damian? Thanks for phoning.'

I put the phone down, dazed. Mum's smile is real this time, from one ear to the other.

'Oh Nicky, he sounds so sweet. Now look, after you go shopping together go to McDonald's, right?'

'But Mum, I can't. You'll be waiting.'

'And I can wait a bit longer. I just want you to have a little bit of fun, sweetheart. Goodness knows, you deserve it. You have to do so much for me.'

'And I always will, Mum,' I say.

I give her a big hug and just at this moment I'm so happy I feel strong enough to scoop her up out of danger and whirl her round and round and keep her flying forever.

Louise Rennison
Big Red Bottomosity
(from the diary
of Georgia Nicolson)

R.E.

1.30 p.m.

Oh no, my head is going to fall off with embarrasmentosity. We are having a 'Sex and relationship' talk. Conducted by the least likely person in the world to have either: Miss Wilson. Knitted woman with a tragic bob. We all tried to get to the back of the classroom and put our fingers in our ears.

It was EXCRUCIATING! First of all, we were shown a film about ovaries and sperm and so on, which was enough to put you off sex for life. Additionally, the woman in the film looked like Meat Loaf. It was really giving me the mega droop. Although I noticed Miss Wilson making notes. Erlack. This is sooooo not right. If I had a bag I would put it on my head. I wonder if I could get my head down my jumper sleeve.

5 mins later

Rosie sent round a note:

To whom it may concern.

You have to choose one of these.

Which would you rather?

1. Elvis Attwood gets to number seven with you. Heavy tongues are involved. He is in the nuddy-pants.

or

2. No snogging ever again.

Pass it on.

And we all had to put one or two. Everyone put two. The thought of Elvis getting to number seven (upper body fondling – outdoors) has made my nunga-nungas quiver with fear.

The next note was:

Which would you rather?

1. Miss Stamp the 'sports' mistress rubs you down with a towel in the showers.

or

2. No snogging ever again.

When we got the results back I was very alarmed to see that Jas had put number one. I whispered to Jas, 'What kind of snacks have you got, lezzie?'

Miss Wilson is now talking to us about sex. Noooooooo. I

am gazing at her knees, which look like elepoon knees. I personally think if you can't even put your tights on properly, you are not likely to be tiptop in the snogging department. She raved and stuttered on about the 'beauty of a fulfilling and caring relationship with someone you love'. Heavens to Betsy. For light relief, Rosie coloured all her teeth black with her fibretip pen which was very funny. (And much funnier later when she couldn't get it off.) At the end, when we were all trying to get out and do a bit of mad dancing and hand washing to release our pent up madnosity, Miss Wilson gave us an egg each. Cheers. Just what I've always wanted.

4.10 p.m.

On the way home. With my new eggy friend. Apparently we have to take care of the egg and look after it and treat it like a tiny baldy baby. It is supposed to teach us about caring and nurturing. I tell you what it is teaching me already and this is it. The whole thing is typically what school is like: totally sad. And useless. And also *très merde*.

8.30 p.m.

I annoyed Vati by telling him that the programme he was watching on TV was unsuitable for my egg. Which, by the way, I have dressed in an old bootie of my little sister Libby's.

I think I may very well be an unusually good mother.

*Egg*cellent, in fact.

Saturday November 20th

2.45 p.m.

Saturday night is party night at Rosie's house.

I've asked Mum to babysit my egg. It will make a change for her to nurture her caring skills. Which she hasn't got.

The ace gang are all going to be there tonight. (Well, apart from Jas, who is going to her so-called boyfriend's parents. Yipppeeeee, what larks she will have . . . not).

Robbie (The Sex God) said he might come round to Rosie's if he could after the family do. I feel sheer desperadoes to see him again. It's been ages since I saw him. Oh well, if he doesn't turn up I can still have fun. I can release my inner Funnosity.

I wonder who will turn up tonight? Rosie and Sven, of course, Mabs and Steve, Jools and Rollo, Ellen and Dave the Laugh . . . Sara, Patty and me . . . and maybe some of Dave the Laugh's mates.

I'm sort of looking forward to it. It will take my mind off my jelloidness about the SG. Even though I will be, as per usual, the goosegog in the manger.

Rosie's house

8.20 p.m.

Sven opened the door wearing a Durex on his head like a hat.

''Ello, welcome to the fish party!'

What was he going on about?

When we went into the living room, it was all full of netting and paper fish hanging up.

Rosie was wearing a really crap mermaid's outfit (her legs down one leg of her blue trousers) and hobbling around. She said, 'Cod evening.'

Good grief.

Actually, it was quite funny. There were fishfingers as snacks. Dave the Laugh arrived with his mates. Ellen was really giddy, but I was cool as a mackerel. Sven said, 'Let's dance,' and we had to dance to fish-type music. The music from *Jaws*. And *Titanic* and so on. And had to dance like fish. Which is not as easy as you would think, because fish aren't big dancers.

Dave was making me laugh because he really did look like a fish dancing! He even said, 'This dancing is playing haddock with my jeans.'

Then we played sardines – well, we played Sven's version of it, which meant that essentially we all got into the wardrobe and some people snogged. And no I am not naming names. What goes on in the wardrobe stays in the wardrobe.

But I'll just say this much, it was Rollo and Jools, and Sven and Rosie. I was a bit too close to Dave the Laugh for my liking. At one point he had to put his arm round me to stop falling over. It almost made me pucker up in the dark . . .

Oh, stop it, stop it. What is it about Dave the Laugh? Ever since we got told about lady baboons getting big red bottoms (to let the slightly dim boy baboons know that they are 'in the mood'), I have developed big red bottomosity. Usually round Dave. Oh nooooo, now I have thought of it, I can feel my bottom getting redder and redder and bigger. I must not, MUST NOT get the big red bottom.

9.20 p.m.

Back in the living room, about to play Truth, Dare, Kiss or Promise. Then the doorbell rang. It was Jas (Mrs Big Knickers herself) and Tom. No Sex God though.

I said to Jas quietly, 'Where is Robbie?'

And she said, 'Who?' Not really listening, just mooning about over Tom. Pathetico. God, she is so annoying.

I said quietly, 'Jas, did he say he was coming?'

A simple enough question, you might have thought, even for Pantshead herself. But no. In front of the whole room she said, loudly, 'You know when you did ear snogging with him? Well, what number is that, snogging scale-wise? Is it after tongues?'

What is the matter with her?! If anyone wants to know anything about my life, all they have to do is to tune into Radio Jas.

9.30 p.m.

Hahahaha. Revenge! Jas got 'Dare' from me and I dared her to fill her knickers up with all the legumes in the vegetable basket. She was grumbling, but in the end she had to do it and went off to the kitchen.

I almost died with laughing when she came back. She had two pounds of potatoes, four carrots and a swede down her knickknacks. And they were not full!

Rosie got 'Truth' and had to tell the truth about what number she and Sven had got up to on the snogging scale. It was . . . eight! They had got up to number eight. Upper body fondling – indoors. Honestly! It gave me quite a turn. Rosie wasn't embarrassed or anything. Then Steve got 'Dare' and he had to eat a raw onion.

Uh-oh, my turn.

Jas got her own back for the vegetable knicker extravaganza in a really horrible way. I got 'Truth', and she said, 'Do you fancy anyone besides the Sex God?'

Dave the Laugh looked at me. Everyone looked at me. What was I? A looking-at thing?

I said, 'Er . . . well, I quite fancy . . . er, Henri. The erm, the Froggy language student teacher.' Phew.

That got them talking about Henri and his trousers. The game went on and then Dave the Laugh got 'Kiss.'

Jools said, 'Okay, Dave, you have to kiss . . .'

Ellen went all pink and incredibly girlish. God, she loves him. She will never get to snog him though, because she will dither her own head off first. But then Jools said, 'Dave the Laugh, you have to kiss . . . Georgia.'

Why did she say that? What did she know? Was my big red bottom showing through my skirt?

33

While everyone went, 'Snog, snog, snog!', I went into the kitchen to get myself a drink.

I was in a state of confusiosity. I wished I knew what I wanted. I wanted everything.

I wanted the Sex God and Dave the Laugh, and also possibly Henri.

Good Lord. I really was a nymphowhatsit.

That is when Dave the Laugh came into the kitchen.

'Georgia.'

'What?'

'You owe me a snog.'

Oh God's pyjamas! I was the girlfriend of a Sex God. I would just have to say, 'No, Dave, the game is over.'

And that is when I accidentally snogged him.

Oh, my lips had no discipline! They were bad, bad lips! Then he stopped, mid-nip libbling, and said, 'Georgia, we shouldn't be doing this.'

That was what I was going to say!

He said, 'Look, I really, really like you. I always have, you know that. But I am not an idiot, you like Robbie and, you know, other girls like me. They are only human – you've seen my dancing . . .'

That made me laugh even amidst the dramatosity.

He went on, because I seemed to be paralysed from the nose downwards. Well, from the neck upwards and the nose downwards.

'But you choose. I would choose you, but you have to

choose. You go for a Sex God or you go for me, who really likes you and who you could have a great time with.'

Then he gave me a little soft kiss on the mouth and went back into the living room.

Midnight

In my bed. With my egg child tucked up next to me. I am beyond the Valley of the Confused and treading lightly in the Universe of the Severely Deranged. *Sacré* bloody *bleu*. I am supposed to be thinking about make-up and my nunga-nungas. Not life-changing decisions. And egg babies. Why can't I just be left alone? Why do I have to care about everything? I'm only fourteen. I only first snogged someone a few months ago and now I'm practically married and have an egg child.

Jas hasn't got red-bottomosity, so it's all very well for her to be boring.

But my bottom demands to be heard.

1.00 a.m.

Oh *sacré* bloody *bleu*. I can't sleep.
Sex God or the Laugh?
Or both.

1.15 a.m.

Jelloid knickers or strange dancing?
Ear snogging or nip libbling?
It is a stark choice.

1.20 a.m.

I wonder what sort of snogging Henri does. Perhaps *les français* do other things that are not on the English snogging scale. Nose libbling, *peut-être*. That might be quite nice.

1.30 a.m.

Nose libbling???!!!!

What am I talking about???!!!!

Sunday November 21st

10.45 a.m. At breakfast.

I think I'm going mad. I feel so bonkers that at this rate I might be driven to ask advice from my mutti. That is how sheer desperadoes I am.

I went into the kitchen and I began to say, 'Mutti, I have a . . .' but then I was so astonished I forgot what I was going to say. For once in her life, Mum had actually made breakfast for me and sister Libbs. Boiled eggs and soldiers. Amazing. And she was practically fully dressed. It was almost like being in a real family. Possibly. I tapped the top of my egg and scooped a bit out, and Mum said, 'Georgia, don't let Libby take eggs in your bed. I found that one on your pillow.'

I was eating my own child.

That is the kind of person I have become.

A red-bottomed child eater.

What could be worse than that?

Then something worse did happen.

Dad came in – in his leather trousers.

Oh, and he also said that Mr Across the Road's pedigree cat is pregnant.

Actually, what he said was, 'Christ on a bike, Naomi is up the duff.'

In my room
Midday
In my bed of pain.

I can still see the little indent in the pillow where my egg child spent so many happy hours.

Who is Naomi pregnant by? They can't blame my cat Angus because we were forced to take him to the vet for the . . . well, you know, the . . . erm, removal of the trouser snake addendum scenario.

3 mins later
Have Angus's missing addendums made a surprise reappearance?

Or has he been cuckolded by Naomi, the little minx?

Perhaps Vati is right that all women are fickle. My own mutti said she liked being a double-dater. And she thrusts her nungas at our hunky local doctor whenever she sees him. And now Naomi has allowed her girlie parts to flow free and wild. She has displayed appalling red-bottomosity.

But how can I point the finger of shame? I am just the same. (Well, not dark brown and with fur, but apart from that.)

1 min later

No, I am much worse.

Much, much worse.

I am a red-bottomed child eater.

Oh *merde*.

The End.

4.00 p.m.

However, on the bright-side, God wouldn't have made me a red bottom in the first place unless he was trying to tell me something. He is, as we all know, impotent. (Or do I mean omnipotent? I don't know, but anyway he is some kind of potent.) Perhaps he is saying, 'Go forth, Georgia, and use your red bottom wisely.'

Hmmmm. So maybe I could have the Sex God AND Dave the Laugh?

And perhaps, for diplomatic world-relationship-type stuff, Henri as well?

Cor, it's all go!

Cathy Hopkins
Mum Never Did Learn To Knock

There was a hammering on the bathroom door.

'Emily, who are you talking to in there?' called Dad.

'Speak later, Mum. Don't worry, I'm on the case. I'll find out what I can,' I whispered into my mobile phone, then quickly flipped it shut. I opened the bathroom door with my best innocent smile. 'No one. Just cleaning my teeth.'

Dad didn't look convinced. 'I heard you,' he insisted. 'You were talking to your mother again, weren't you?'

'No.'

'Well, you were talking to someone.'

I waved my phone at him. 'Lou. I was talking to Lou, that's all,' I said. 'Homework thingy. So, what's for supper?' *Change*

39

the subject fast, I thought as Dad's expression showed concern. 'Takeaway or takeaway? I fancy pizza. Four cheeses. Okay?'

We've lived on takeaways since Mum left. I did attempt to try and cook at first, but wasn't too good at it besides cheese on toast, and Dad can only do rubbery scrambled eggs. Yuck.

Dad put his hand on my shoulder. 'Emily . . . would you . . . would you like to talk to someone?'

'Some*one*?'

'A counsellor.'

'Like who? Not Aunt Iz, *puleese*. She lives in wacko land.'

Aunt Iz is Dad's barmy younger sister and calls herself a new-age counsellor. All kinds of people go to her for healing-schmealing, and she consults the Tarot and stars on their behalf and advises them to drink disgusting-tasting herbs. So Aunt Iz? No, ta. Mum and I used to joke that she was a witch.

'No, no, I mean a *proper* counsellor,' said Dad. 'There are people who specialise in . . . situations like ours.'

So now he thinks I need help, I thought. *Just because I've stayed in touch with Mum. I wish he'd see her or talk to her at least. She's looking great now. Loads better than before she left. Dad's the one who ought to see a counsellor. He's the one who's bottled everything up and thrown himself into his work so that he doesn't have to think about what happened.*

'No thanks, Dad,' I said. 'I'm fine. And I'll . . . I've stopped talking to her.' *Liar, liar pants on fire,* I thought, *but what else am I to do? I'm not having people thinking I'm bonkers just because I want to talk to my mum.*

Dad looked at the floor and shifted awkwardly. 'It's not just me, Em,' he said. 'Miss Doolie phoned from the school last night. They're worried about you there, too. Said you've been behaving strangely – and it seems that you saw your mother at school.'

Well, I'm not likely to turn her away, I thought, *not now that she needs me.*

'Miss Doolie has arranged for you to see the school counsellor on Monday at lunchtime . . .'

'Oh Da-*ad*. Gimme a break. I told you I've stopped talking to her, so I don't see what the problem is. Look, no way do I need to see a counsellor. That's for saddos.'

Dad pressed my shoulder. 'Do it for me, kid. I know these past weeks have been tough on you.'

It won't be so bad, I told myself the following Monday as I set off to see the counsellor. *She's probably one of those old hippie types like Aunt Iz, all long flowing Afghan skirts and big ethnic beads. I'll just say what she wants to hear and have her eating out of my hand.* Aunt Iz was a pushover as long as you agreed to be open-minded and let her wave a crystal or two over you.

As I sat waiting in the corridor, Mark Riley and Andrew Derrington walked past.

'All right, Potts?' called Andrew. 'In to see the shrink, are you? What you done? Wet your bed? Gone potty? Hey that's good, Emily Potts has gone potty.'

'Get lost, potato head,' I replied with as much disdain as I could muster. 'Actually, I'm here because they're thinking of transferring me to a school for gifted pupils. They're worried that my natural talent is being held back because I have to mix with bozos like you.'

Mark cracked up. He fancies me, I know he does. He told Avril Jeffries in Year Nine and she told Lou, and Lou told me. And he's okay for a boy. Cute-looking with no spots. He laughs easily too. I like that.

'You? Gifted? Yeah right,' said Andrew. 'You definitely need help.'

At that moment, my mobile bleeped and luckily the boys moved off so I could answer. It was Mum.

'Hey, Emily, sorry I haven't been in touch since Saturday. I'm still trying to adjust, you know . . .'

'I've been summoned to see a counsellor, Mum. Everyone thinks I'm losing the plot because of you so I'm going to have to be careful about talking to you from now on . . . A lot of people don't understand.'

'Funny, isn't it? If anyone needs a counsellor at the moment,' she said, 'it's me. No one prepares you for this, and I really don't know what I'm supposed to do next. It was so easy with your father. He always knew what to do.'

'So why haven't you tried talking to him?'

'Oh I have,' she snorted. 'Don't think I haven't tried, but he's not receptive. He just blanks me. It's like I've become invisible to him.'

'His way of dealing with it. You know how he likes to keep things in separate boxes. That was then, this is now, kind of thing.'

'I know, love,' she said. 'Thank God I still have you.'

The door opened and the school secretary stuck her head out.

'You can go in now, Emily. Mrs Armstrong is waiting.'

'Catch you later,' I said to Mum as I got up and flipped my phone shut.

Inside the room was dingy and it smelled musty, like no one had opened the windows in years. Around a battered coffee table were three chairs that looked like they'd come off a skip – one orange, one brown and one flowery – and on top of the table was a large box of tissues. *People must do a lot of crying in here,* I thought as a tall white-haired lady got up to greet me.

'You must be Emily Potts,' she said as she offered me her hand.

I nodded. I'd give my name away but nothing else.

'Take a seat,' she said, pointing at a chair.

I did as I was told and sat opposite her.

'I'm Mrs Armstrong,' she said, 'but you can call me Gloria.'

She was nothing like I expected. She was wearing a navy blue tailored suit with high heels. She looked more like a business lady than a touchy-feely-type-helper out to heal the world.

'You the counsellor?' I asked.

She nodded. 'I am. Is that okay?'

I shrugged. 'I guess.'

She glanced down at a book of notes, then back up at me. 'So Emily, let's get down to business,' she said. 'Now. Do you want to tell me a little about yourself.'

No, but I thought I'd better make some kind of effort. Hmm. What to say to keep her off the Mum trail?

'Um. Usual,' I said. 'Five foot two at the last count but still growing, I hope. Medium build. Wish I was taller, wish I was thinner. I like art and English. Don't like the colour of my hair. Dad calls it chestnut, but I think it's boring and I'd like some highlights, but he won't let me. Dunno. Usual stuff.'

Gloria didn't seem that interested, but she made a few notes in her book, then looked back up at me. 'Yes. I can see what you look like, Emily. What I meant to ask is, what's been going on with you lately?'

I shrugged again. 'Nothing. Same old, same old.'

Gloria didn't smile. 'I see,' she said and made another note in her book. 'So . . . why do you think you've been sent to see me?'

I shrugged. 'Dunno.'

'Okay, so how do feel about seeing me?'

'Dunno. Okay, I suppose.' Silence from Gloria so I thought I'd better add something. 'How do *you* feel about seeing me?'

'I feel good about seeing you,' said Gloria in a soft voice that made me feel like throwing up. *Why do people feel they have to be quiet around me now and treat me with kid gloves? It's not like what's happened is a first.* 'But I'm concerned. Your teachers have told me about your mother.'

'Have they?'

'They have,' said Gloria, followed by another long silence.

'What about her?'

Gloria coughed and shifted in her seat. 'That she . . . she died three weeks ago.'

'Yeah. So?'

'Well, I'm told that you talk to her. I know, nothing wrong with that. A lot of people in your situation do, but you do know that she's dead, don't you?'

Another looooong silence. I wondered if I was supposed to pitch in, or was she waiting for me to break down and cry – hence the tissues.

It was Gloria who cracked and spoke first. 'I wonder . . . how do feel about that?' she asked, in a voice so soft you could hardly hear her.

I felt like laughing. *How do I feel about that? Oh, over the moon, Gloria. It's great to see your mum fade away in front of you. Best time of my life. Not.*

'How do you think I feel?' I asked, carefully omitting the words 'you dingbat' that I was thinking.

'Are you aware you keep asking *me* questions, Emily?'

'Are you aware that you keep asking me questions, Gloria?' *I mean, asking if I knew Mum was dead and how did I feel about it,* I thought, *how stupid can you get?* Of course I know Mum's dead. I was at her funeral. Okay, it didn't sink in right away, as

45

before that she'd always been there, every day, since I was born. I know that's obvious, but not everybody in your life has been there all the time from the start.

It didn't seem real when she died. Couldn't be true. Like she'd gone to the hospital for a few days and would walk back in through the door at any moment.

At first, I took Dad's attitude – kept myself busy, tried to cook a bit, cleaned the house, did the washing and stuff. Tried to shut out the enormity of it. It wasn't like her death was unexpected. She'd been ill for almost a year and we'd had long chats about how it would be when she'd gone. She was so organised about it all. Even down to choosing the music, flowers and readings for her funeral. She was like that, Mum. Mrs Efficient.

Then, on the fourth day, it hit me that she really wasn't coming back this time. I was in the downstairs cloakroom and it still smelled of her perfume. She always kept a bottle down there. Ô de Lancôme. Light. Lemony. I realised that the scent would fade as Mum had. I sat on the loo and reached for a piece of toilet paper, only to find that the roll had finished and there wasn't any more in the cupboard under the sink where she usually kept it. It was then that it hit home. My mum really had gone. There was no one to buy the loo rolls anymore. There was no one to take care of me anymore.

I sat there and sobbed my heart out. It felt like a dam had burst inside of me, and all the feelings I'd been holding back came flooding out, bringing with them a thousand questions. And the biggest one was, where had she gone? I realised that in all the chats we'd had about her dying and about me coping afterwards, she'd never once mentioned where she would be going. I couldn't believe we hadn't discussed it. She always left a note stuck on the fridge door when she went anywhere, even out to the shops for ten minutes. I went into the kitchen to double check. But no, nothing. Only a Santa magnet from last Christmas. I opened the back door and yelled with all my strength into the night sky, 'WHERE ARE YOU? M–*UM*. WHERE HAVE YOU GONE?'

A curtain twitched next-door and I heard a window open, so I whispered it again, '*Where have you gone?*' I kept asking myself over and over again. *Where do people go when they die?* So when Gloria asked if I realised that she was dead, the answer is *Yes, oh most definitely yes.*

Gloria was still staring at me, waiting for me to say something or break down, but I'd had enough. There was nothing Gloria could say or do to help me. One thing I knew for sure though and that was that I didn't want to be coming to counselling every week for the next month. I had to bluff my way out.

'So, this talking to your mother . . .' Gloria started.

'Listen, Mrs Arm— Gloria,' I said. 'Yes, I do talk to Mum. It makes me feel better, like she can hear me somewhere, wherever she is. Like she's not really gone. I'm not mad or disturbed or anything. I'm cool. I know she's dead.'

Gloria looked at me sympathetically. 'It must have been very hard for you.'

I nodded. 'Yeah.' I wanted out of there to hang out with Mark. After assembly this morning, he'd asked what I was doing at lunchtime and even hinted that we could walk home together. 'But I'm okay, I've got my dad. And Mum told me she'd be watching over me and I could always talk to her. That's why I do it. I'm not loony petuni or anything. I'll be okay. I'm coping.'

Gloria nodded and made a few notes on her pad. I think I had her convinced that I wasn't out of my mind, and she was just getting ready to round up our session, when Mum came in through the door. And I mean literally, right through the door. Cool, that.

'All right, love?' she asked as she hovered behind Gloria.

I nodded and motioned her to be quiet. Not that Gloria would see or hear her. Seems like it's only me that does that, but I didn't want to react or anything. I didn't want Gloria clocking that I wasn't just *talking* to Mum. I could *see* her. If Gloria thought that, then she'd definitely think I was unhinged and I'd have to come back to counselling another time.

'I was just thinking,' said Mum, as Gloria put her notebook into her bag. 'Could you ask her if she knows where I'm supposed to go?'

'Um, Gloria, just one more thing,' I said as Gloria got up.

Gloria smiled and sat again. 'Yes, Emily.'

'Er, where *do* people go when they die? I mean, where will Mum be? What happens when you die?'

Gloria paled. 'Er, well . . . that's a big question.'

'I know. Do you have the answer?'

Gloria looked at her watch. 'I'm afraid we're out of time Emily. Um. So many big questions in life – let me get back to you on that.'

Mum stood next to me and we both studied Gloria, hoping that she was going to say something. After a while, Mum shook her head. 'I don't think she knows, love.'

'Neither do I,' I said.

'Pardon?' said Gloria.

'Oh. Nothing. Was just thinking, neither do I know where they go. Can I leave now?'

Gloria nodded. 'Unless there's anything else.'

I couldn't resist. 'Just one more question, if you don't mind.'

Gloria was beginning to look distinctly worried. 'Go ahead.'

'What's after space?'

Mum burst out laughing, as it was the question I used to drive her mad with when I was junior school.

Gloria looked like she couldn't wait to get out of the room. 'My but you're a curious child,' she said. 'Er. Can I get back to you on that as well?'

'Sure,' I said. 'Take all the time you need.'

Gloria got up and hurried out of the room.

'Seems nobody knows,' said Mum when she'd gone.

'Seems like. Sorry, Mum, but I told you, I'll do my best to find out.'

After the meeting with Gloria, Mum hung around for the rest of the afternoon. It was a blast, especially when she peeked at Mr Parker's notes, then gave me all the answers for my history test. First time ever that I got an A. After school, she didn't seem to be in a hurry to be off anywhere, and who could blame her – she didn't know where to go. She said she needed to be around someone she knew, and no way was she hanging out at the cemetery where she was buried. 'There are dead people in there,' she said, then we both cracked up laughing.

It was brilliant having her around, and we joked about the fact that we spent more time together now she was dead than when she was alive. And it was easy to talk to her without attracting attention, as I simply got my phone out and pretended I was talking to someone on the other end.

The rest of the week, we did the mall and a movie, where Mum realised that there were some perks to being a ghostie, as she got in without paying. We went to the library; she even sat at the back of most of my classes at school. It was hard not to burst out laughing when she shouted out answers to questions and harrumphed loudly if a teacher said anything she didn't approve of.

I did try and confide in my best mate, Lou, but she didn't want to know. I think she's gone into the 'Emily has lost the plot' camp, no matter how much I tell her that it's cool. She's terrified of ghosts.

'Mum says ghosts aren't scary,' I told her. 'They're the same as normal people . . .'

'Duh, yeah, only one small difference,' said Lou, 'like, they're dead.'

She wasn't having any of it. It's probably because she watches so many horror films, so she thinks that ghosts are all terrifying. I know different now. Mum said that just because you die, you don't have a personality change. She says it's fear, fear of the unknown that scares people. *Scares ghosts too,* I thought, but she's right about it being the unknown. It's weird. Death happens to everyone, and yet no one wants to talk about it, and no one really seems to know what happens.

Not that I wasn't scared when Mum first showed up. I was terrified. I was in the bath, the night after I'd been shouting my lungs out in the back garden, and suddenly she came floating out of the airing cupboard. Just like that. Dressed just how she used to be in real life, in her old blue tracksuit and trainers. My first reaction was to scream and close my eyes to make her go away, but when I opened them, there she was standing there at the side of the bath. We got talking, and that's when the trouble started and people began to think that I was disturbed and wasn't accepting her death. Of course it wasn't that. I knew she was dead and wasn't coming back as she was before. But she was there in another form, no doubt about that, and she needed my help.

Sadly, our research into the afterlife only seemed to confuse things. There was a wealth of material out there – sites on the internet, books and magazines from the wonderful to the weird. Priests, gurus, philosophers, mystics, rabbis, all with their opinion-schminions.

'What we need,' said Mum, 'is a sort of guide book. An A-Z of the afterlife, sort of thing.'

'Probably have it in W.H.Smith's,' I joked. 'They sell maps. If not, we could always go back to the internet and type *afterlife maps* into Google.'

But we found nothing really useful anywhere – zilch. I didn't care. It was great having her around.

One night after school, Mark was waiting for me by the bus stop.

'All right, Potts?'

'Yeah. You?'

'Yeah.'

Hmm. So far a fascinating conversation – not, I thought, and decided to take the plunge.

'Hey, Riley. You believe in ghosts?'

'I would if I saw one, but I haven't, so can't say.'

'But you don't *not* believe?'

'No. Who knows? Why you seen one?'

'Yeah. My mum.'

'Get out of here. When?'

'All the time. She's always popping up.'

'She all green and slimy?'

I sighed. Another person who wasn't taking me seriously. 'No,' I said. 'She looks like Mum. But see-through. She smells different though. Not like her old perfume anymore. Her smell always arrives a moment before she does. It's divine, like a garden of roses in summer.'

'Way to go, Potts. She around now?'

'No, but she probably will be later – that is, if she's not gone to see a movie.'

Mark looked at me as if I was mad. I guess it did sound a bit strange. Not your usual conversation with a boy you fancy. But then he smiled. 'Why not?' he said. 'Yeah. Cool.'

'So you don't think I'm mad?'

He shook his head. 'No. I've often wondered where people go when they die. My dog Petra died last year. It was awful. I mean, I know she was only a dog but she was like my best mate. I'd had her all my life. She always slept on the end of my bed. And then she wasn't there anymore. I read everything I could about what happens next. Read up a lot about ghosts.'

'So why do they stay around? I've been checking it out on the net, but everyone seems to contradict each other.'

'Apparently,' said Mark, 'ghosts hang around for two reasons. One, they died in a traumatic way and are in shock, like they haven't quite adjusted to the fact they're dead —'

'That's not Mum. She knew she was dying for about a year.'

'And two, unfinished business.'

'Like what?'

'Dunno. Left the oven on. Something not said or done. Something to clear up with someone still down here. Feeling responsible for someone they've left behind. So why do you reckon your ma's still around?'

I shrugged, but I was beginning to have an inkling.

'What exactly did happen when you left your body?' I asked Mum later that evening, when she turned up in my bedroom.

'Ooh, it was lovely,' she said. 'I'd been drifting up a tunnel and floated out at the end into an ocean of white light. I felt surrounded by love and warmth. It felt like going home. I can't ever remember feeling so at peace. Then, suddenly, I had this terrible feeling that I'd forgotten something. Before I knew it, I felt myself being tugged earthwards, and found myself coming through the bathroom wall, and there you were. In the buff, in the bath.'

'I know. You never did learn to knock,' I said.

Mum grinned. 'I would have if I could,' she said putting her hand through the wall for emphasis.

'I . . . I think I know why you came back. It was me crying out for you. It was when I realised that you'd really gone. I felt such an overpowering sense of being alone, I was devastated. I think I brought you back. I was shouting out, *Where are you?* because you'd forgotten to tell me where you were going. And I really missed you . . . and I wanted you back . . . I . . . I didn't know at the time what would happen.'

Mum tried to put her arm round me, but it kept going through me, so she held it a short distance away, as though she was giving me a hug.

'I know, love. I'm sorry I couldn't let you know. Just . . . I didn't know at the time. But it seemed that I was going somewhere very nice. It really felt . . . oh, I can't describe it, but it was a good place.' Then her face clouded, which is a strange look on someone who's transparent. Like a glass bowl that's steamed up. 'But now I fear I might have missed the boat, or the ride, or whatever it was.'

'No. It can't be like that. Like boarding a plane and if you miss your flight, you can't go. It can't be.'

Mum shrugged. 'Ah well. No doubt it will get sorted. So what are we doing tonight?'

'Ah . . .' Mark was coming over and I was hoping to see him on his own. I had a feeling that he wanted to kiss me but didn't want to do it in front of her, and who could blame him? Dead or alive, having your mother as an audience for a first kiss is uncool in anyone's book.

Luckily, I was saved from hurting Mum's feelings by someone ringing the doorbell downstairs.

'It's your Aunt Iz,' Dad called up the stairs a few moments later.

'Maybe you'd better go,' I said to Mum as she looked out of the window, hoping for a glimpse of Dad's sister.

'No way,' she said. 'I wouldn't miss this for the world.'

We made our way downstairs, me walking, Mum floating behind me like Mary Poppins, and we found Aunt Iz in the kitchen. She'd brought a dish of orange gloop which she put on the table.

'A nice healthy lentil roast,' she said, when she saw me looking. 'I was worried you weren't eating properly.'

Mum pulled an I'm-going-to-be sick face behind her. She'd never liked Aunt Iz's cooking either.

Over supper, we chatted about school and talked a little about Mum's death. I had a really hard time keeping a straight face, as the whole time, Mum was looning about the kitchen making mad faces and doing her impersonation of an Egyptian dancer in the air. That did it and I sprayed a mouthful of lentils everywhere and almost choked. I think Aunt Iz thought my hysteria was down to me being seriously disturbed about Mum's passing, and so when we'd cleared away the dishes, she suggested we had a séance to try and contact Mum, so that she could reassure me that she was okay. She roped in Dad too. At first he was reluctant, as he's not into any of that heebie-jeebie stuff, as he calls it, but I talked him round and he agreed, if only to stop Aunt Iz fussing.

We lit candles, sat at the kitchen table, and after a few minutes, Aunt Iz started swaying and rolling her eyeballs.

I had to bite my cheeks to stop myself from laughing, and I could see Dad trying not to smile.

'I think . . . I'm . . . m-making contact,' said Aunt Iz in a strange deep voice as Mum floated past and stuck a finger up her nose.

Of course, that set me off again and my shoulders started to shake with suppressed laughter. And then Dad got the giggles, even though he couldn't see what was really going on. Mum was on a roll. She floated in and out through the pantry door. Then she'd disappear altogether and just stick her leg through then back again, then her arm in and out, then finally her bum. By this time, I was on the floor laughing which soon snapped Aunt Iz out of her trance. And Dad had tears of laughter rolling down his cheeks at the sight of me desperately trying to keep it together and failing miserably.

'If neither of you are going to take me seriously, I'm leaving,' she said, then stomped off and out of the front door in a huff.

After she'd gone, Dad and I looked at each other.

'More lentils, dear?' he sniggered.

'No, ta,' I said, and we burst out laughing again.

Dad looked sad for a moment. 'I think your mum would have enjoyed that,' he said.

I put my hand over his. 'Maybe she was watching us from where ever she is,' I said.

'Maybe,' said Dad softly.

Mum winked at me from behind him, then let her hand rest gently over his shoulder.

For a few weeks, we continued to have more fun, but the novelty of seeing Mum appear and disappear was beginning to wear thin. I was seeing more and more of Mark. And that was the problem. Mum kept popping up at inappropriate moments to ask awkward questions:

'How long have you known this boy?'

'Aren't you a little young for a relationship?'

'Are you serious about him?'

'Mum, I don't want to talk to you about him.'

We could never get any time on our own.

And the lack of privacy was beginning to get to me, like her coming out of the bath plug when I was in the bath, or out of my knicker drawer when I was getting changed. Or waking me up early in the morning because she was bored and wanted someone to talk to.

In the meantime, Mark helped me do my research into the afterlife. It seemed that a lot of people had had near-death experiences like Mum's when their heart had stopped on the operating table, or they'd had a car accident or something, but they'd later come round to tell the tale. All of them seemed happy about dying since their near-death experience – in fact some said they were quite looking forward to it when it happened properly, as they now felt sure that there was somewhere wonderful to go to. Most of them said that they now believed that the physical body was nothing more than a shell that houses the real self. And Mum had to agree. She had no worries about going 'back up there' either.

One night after school, Mark and I walked home through the park and we stopped at the old elm tree by the railings.

He put his arms round me and I snuggled in.

'Is she around?' he asked.

I sniffed the air for her rose smell and shook my head.

He titled my chin up and leaned in to kiss me. *Get ready to pucker,* I thought, as I glanced over his shoulder to make sure that there weren't any nosy neighbours around, ready to report back to Dad.

Suddenly the air filled with roses and Mum appeared on the other side of the railings.

I leapt back.

'What's up?' asked Mark. 'Don't you want to?'

'No. Just . . .'

'Ah. Your mum showed?'

I nodded. 'Mu*uum* . . .' I began.

Mum looked particularly radiant. 'Won't be a minute, sunshine,' she said. 'Just wanted to check you're all right.'

'Yeeesss, I'm fine,' I said, rolling my eyes. 'Look, Mum, much as I love you, you can't keep popping up everywhere unannounced. I do have my own life you know and . . . bit of a private moment here . . .'

'I know, love,' she said softly. 'We've both got to move on. And . . . well . . . I . . . I think I'm ready to go now.'

She smiled at me and gently brushed my cheek with her hand. Part of me wanted to yell, *Noooooo, not yet, just a little longer,* but I knew it was time. I had to let her go. I smiled back and nodded.

And then she was gone. I inhaled the last lingering scent of roses as Mark wrapped me in his arms.

I never did see her again. But I still talk to her sometimes, and I'm sure she can hear, wherever she's gone. And I don't feel worried anymore, as I'm sure it's somewhere good.

And sometimes, just sometimes, like on my birthday, or days that for some reason I have the blues, I smell the scent of roses and know that she's not too far away. She's some place watching over me, and wherever it is, she's happy.

Meg Cabot
Digger Number 5

The interrogation started before I had a chance to sit down.

'What's your name?' she demanded.

'Helen,' I said, blinking.

'*Helen?*' She raised her perfectly waxed eyebrows. 'You're kidding me, right?'

'Um,' I said. 'No, I'm not. Helen Regis Whemple. My dad named me after my mom, Helen Regis. She died giving birth to me. She, uh, used to go here.'

If I thought that was going to win me any sympathy points, it turned out I was sadly mistaken.

'Whatever,' she said, rolling her heavily made-up eyes. 'Come this way.'

I should have known: it was an ambush.

Girls with thousand dollar bags do *not* ask the new girl with the Jansport backpack to join them at their lunch table without an ulterior motive – as anyone who has ever been in a high school cafeteria very well knows.

Of course, I'd been living out of a tent in the desert with my dad my whole life. I wouldn't even have realised that a purse could cost a thousand dollars if I hadn't been at Bloomingdales with my grandmother Regis just the day before, trying to pick out a bag for my first day of school. I'd lifted up the very purse Lauren Woodcrest had dangling so casually from her slender shoulder because it seemed like what all the stylish girls I saw on the streets of Manhattan were carrying. Maybe it would help me fit in . . . even make a friend, for a change.

Then I'd looked at the price tag and almost had a heart attack.

I'd gone with a Jansport backpack, over Grandmother Regis's strenuous objections. It just seemed more . . . *me*.

As you can imagine, it was a *huge* hit my first day at the Milton Academy for Girls in New York City.

Not.

The worst part of it was that, even with all the reading I'd done on the plane about American High Schools, I didn't see what was behind Lauren Woodcrest's sudden urge to get to know me.

Not then.

Not until it was almost too late.

There were no formalities whatsoever. As soon as we sat down, Lauren started in with: 'So, Helen Regis Whemple. Where do you live?'

Me: 'Eighty-first and Fifth.'

LW: 'Off Central Park. Across from the Metropolitan Museum of Art? Impressive. I assume that's part of the Regis estate.'

Me: 'No. See, my dad's a professor and he's curating a show that's about to go on display at the museum, so . . .'

LW: '. . . the apartment is on loan while you guys look for your own place?'

Me: 'Yeah.'

A girl seated beside Lauren – who, I feel I should not need to mention, was just as blond and stylish as Lauren was – gasped.

'If your dad is a professor, does that mean you can get us into frat parties?' she wanted to know.

'Shut up, Pamie,' Lauren said. Then, to me, she said, 'Your dad is that professor who's been all over the news because he discovered that Egyptian tomb. The famous one with the mummy of that super rich pharaoh guy in it. Right?'

Obviously I couldn't deny it. It's been on CNN nearly every day.

'Yes,' I said. 'The tomb of King Ankhtika.'

'So, what?' Lauren demanded. 'Were you home-schooled up until now? Is that why you can't accessorise?'

'Uh,' I said, looking down at my Milton Academy uniform. What was wrong with the way I accessorised? Everything, evidently. 'Something like that.'

I saw no need to mention that accessorising had not exactly been high on my list of priorities while being dragged around the desert by my dad as he tried to prove to the snooty Regises that he had been worthy of marrying into their precious family by chasing down his dream 'find' – the one that was going to put him on the cover of *National Geographic* while also guaranteeing him a seat as dean of some prestigious university.

Or the fact that the reason we'd finally left Egypt for New York was because his dream had come true: his 'find' was about to go on display at the Metropolitan Museum, and Dad had just accepted a post as dean of Columbia University's Department of Archaeology.

Pamie, it turned out, had a few questions of her own.

Pamie: 'So do you have a boyfriend?'

Me: 'No.'

Pamie (frustrated): 'Any brothers? Any guy friends at *all* you can introduce us to?'

Me: 'No.'

It was obvious that the ladies at the Milton Academy for Girls, where Grandmother Regis insisted I attend now that Dad had returned to America, were desperate for male companionship.

You're probably wondering why I didn't tell Pamie about

Digger. He does, after all, qualify as a 'guy' under Pamie's somewhat loose definition of the word, which I took to mean single, male, and old enough to grow facial hair.

And Digger Number 5 is definitely my favourite of all of them so far, since he isn't *always* talking about archaeological methodology and research, but actually seems to have a life (and looks so hot in his jeans).

But how to explain Digger to Lauren and Pamie? I could just see myself going, 'The truth is, ladies, my father has always asked his graduate assistants to babysit me, since he's too busy robbing the graves of dead pharaohs to look after me himself. And yes, this *is* kind of inappropriate since I'm seventeen and his latest grad assistant is only twenty-one and also incredibly hot . . . and male. But all I've ever wanted my whole life is a friend my own age . . . a *real* friend. I do *not* need anyone else to take care of me.'

I knew these girls wouldn't get it. They'd block out the geeky grad assistant part and the fact that my dad is *paying* him to take care of me, and think I'm living with Ashton Kutcher.

Except that maybe they *did* hear that, somehow, because the next thing I knew, Lauren was talking.

LW: 'We're coming over to your place tonight.'

Me: 'Wait. What? You *are*?'

I had never been so surprised in my life. Why would Lauren Palmer and her equally stylish (if somewhat boy-crazy) friend Pamie want to come over to see *me*? It certainly wasn't because of my accessories.

Then again, I wasn't going to look this gift horse in the mouth. Here it was, my first day at a new school, and already some cool girls wanted to get to know me!

No way was I not going to let them.

'Okay,' I said, grinning like an idiot.

Yes, I really was just that stupid.

Because I honestly thought Lauren Woodcrest wanted me as a friend. Little did I know my *friendship* was the last thing she wanted.

As soon as I got home from school, I tore around the apartment, fluffing up pillows and filling vases with the fresh flowers I'd bought. Dad wasn't home – he was still at the museum, supervising the uncrating of the artefacts from King Ankhtika's tomb.

But Digger was there. Digger was *always* there.

He watched me race around like a madwoman until finally he said, 'Are you redecorating? Or is a reality TV show coming over to film, and you forgot to tell me?'

'Digger,' I said, putting a bowl of M&Ms out on the coffee table. 'I'm having some friends from school over tonight. You should probably leave.'

'Really?' he asked, looking pained. 'Even in New York, you're going to insist on calling me Digger?'

Me: 'Aren't you an aspiring archaeologist?'

Him: 'You know I am. And yes, archaeologists dig for a

living, among other things. But I'd really prefer it if you'd just call me John.'

Me: 'Whatever you say, Dig. Now get out, if you don't want to be mauled to death by some very boy-crazy high school girls.'

Looking hurt, Digger took his laptop and told me he'd be at the Starbucks around the corner with his mobile on if I needed him. I waved goodbye, pretending not to care.

Except of course I *did* care. That was the problem. I cared *too much*. I'd lied about the real reason why I call him Digger, and not by his real name.

It was just so *hard* to make new friends . . . except the ones your dad pays for, that you just have to say goodbye to forever as soon as they graduate.

So why bother letting myself get to know their real names? Or get attached to them at all?

I didn't like admitting it (I had no one to admit it *to*, since Dad wouldn't understand, and Grandmother Regis would be scandalised at the idea), but John, Digger Number 5, was going to be the hardest one of all to say goodbye to.

It wasn't just that John seemed to have a life outside of Egyptology (and looked so good in his jeans). He seemed to actually think of me as more than just his professor's annoying teenage daughter, and talked to me like an adult, despite my refusing to call him by his real name.

Sometimes I even thought I caught him sneaking looks at me at dinner while Dad was going on about the curse of

Sheeratikirah. (Dad can get really long winded about things like execration texts – ancient Egyptian hieroglyphics written on blocks of stone that bear warnings or lay curses on people. The one over the doorway of King Ankhtika's tomb basically said, *Do not enter, or face the wrath of the spirit of the king's high priestess, Sheeratikirah.* It was there to ward off the graverobbers, and no one but my dad took it seriously.)

But John sneaking adoring looks at me over dinner was probably just my imagination. What guy would look at *me*? As Lauren Woodcrest pointed out, I can't even accessorise.

When John finally graduates and leaves us, I know I'll never recover.

That's why I kept my heart carefully protected in a thick-walled tomb of my own, and made sure never, ever to call John anything but Digger, to remind myself that that's all I can afford to let him be to me: another one of Dad's paid diggers.

Nothing else.

It was getting close to eight o'clock when Lauren and Pamie finally showed up. They'd changed out of their school uniforms (of course), and into very low rise jeans and a lot of shimmery make-up. I wasn't sure why they'd bothered, when it was just going to be us girls.

They looked around. Then Pamie asked, 'So where are the frat guys?'

Now I understood what was going on with the make-up and clothes. Also why they'd come over in the first place.

'Columbia's not a university really known for all that,' I explained, feeling a pain in my heart. 'And we're across the park and about twenty blocks from the actual campus . . .'

Pamie looked disappointed at first, but then resigned. She sat down on the couch and began to dig into the bowl of M&Ms I'd set out.

Lauren, on the other hand, asked, 'Where's your dad, Helen?'

'Oh,' I said. 'He's still over at the museum putting the finishing touches on the King Ankhtika show. It opens next week —'

'Can we go over there now and see it early?' Lauren interrupted.

I was surprised. I hadn't been aware that American teenagers were that interested in Egyptian antiquities.

'Why would we want to do *that*?' Pamie asked, proving that I was right. She dropped some M&Ms in her mouth. 'Unless there are some frat guys there, of course.'

'Because,' Lauren said. 'I want to go tonight.'

I started to get a funny sort of sinking feeling, but it turned out to be for all the wrong reasons.

'I can schedule a private viewing for you with my dad as tour guide,' I said. I tried not to let my hurt feelings show. Of *course* Lauren just wanted to come over for the alleged frat guys . . . or a free peek at King Ankhtika. It wasn't *me* she'd wanted to get to know at all. Why would anyone want to get to know *me* (that my dad wasn't paying)?

But if Lauren wanted to be bored to death as I always was when my dad went on and on about the 'curse of Sheeratikirah,' that was her business.

'But nothing's ready for the public just yet,' I went on. 'It would have to be next —'

'Oh,' Lauren said, her beautifully made-up eyes narrowing. 'No. I'm afraid it will have to be tonight.'

That's when Lauren reached into her thousand dollar handbag and pulled out a shiny, jeweled, gold-handled dagger.

I recognised the dagger right away from similar knives my dad and his various diggers had dug up from the King Ankhtika site.

Before I could move, Lauren grabbed me from behind, then pointed the dagger at my throat.

Then she hissed, 'You're getting me in to see the show now, tonight, so I can re-perform funeral rights on my king, whose tomb has been so heinously and willfully desecrated by your graverobber of a father.'

I couldn't believe I'd been so stupid.

I thought I'd finally made some friends . . . my first real friends ever.

But it turned out I'd been wrong.

As wrong as I could be.

'Whoa,' Pamie said from the couch, looking over at us,

wide-eyed. 'Lauren, what's the matter with you? It's not her fault about the frat guys.'

'I'm not Lauren, you simple fools, but Sheeratikirah,' Lauren said, jabbing the dagger into the soft flesh of my neck. 'The king's high priestess. I'm here to make right the insult that has been wrought against my lord and master – guiding his soul back to its proper resting place and wreaking revenge on those who have disrupted his everlasting sleep. It is my duty! Take me to my king. Now!'

I swallowed. The execration texts written outside King Ankhtika's tomb had warned about this. *Dad* had warned about this, every night at dinner.

But I'd never listened because I'd always been too busy wondering if Digger Number 5 was sneaking peeks at me.

The curse of Sheeratikirah. It was real!

Great. And I'd sent my paid protector to Starbucks to get him out of the way because I'd wanted to have uninterrupted girl bonding time – with Sheeratikirah herself, who had taken over the body of Lauren Woodcrest, the most popular senior at Milton Academy for Girls.

'Oh my God, Lauren,' Pamie said, looking unimpressed from where she still sat on the couch. 'Really? Remember last time? My mom said you really need to cut back on the caffeine.'

But I knew Lauren – the *real* Lauren – wasn't with us anymore. Her soul had been possessed by one that was far more powerful than any high school mean girl.

71

'*Do as I say*,' Sheeratikirah hissed. 'Or you'll feel my wrath!'

I certainly *did* feel it. The dagger's point was piercing my skin.

The funny thing was, the dagger didn't hurt as much as the fact that Lauren and Pamie hadn't come over because they liked me.

They'd come over because they wanted to kill me.

'God, Lauren,' Pamie said, looking annoyed. She took out her mobile and started dialling. 'I'm calling my mom. I'm going to have her come over, *and* bring her medical bag. Because you're acting crazy, just like that time at the TopShop sale. I think you need a vitamin B shot.'

That's when it hit me: *Pamie* didn't want to kill me. *She* wasn't possessed by the spirit of a powerful and long-dead high priestess. She *had* to like me, at least a little, or she wouldn't still be sitting on my couch.

She could have left as soon as she found out there weren't any frat guys hidden in my apartment.

But she hadn't. She'd stayed. And was currently calling her mother, apparently a medical doctor, for support.

'Pamie,' I managed to choke out, as Lauren/Sheeratikirah squeezed my throat with the arm she'd flung around it. 'Hang up, and call this number, and tell the guy who answers what's going on!'

I managed to cough out Digger's number before Sheeratikirah could strangle me back into silence.

'What are you doing?' Sheeratikirah cried. 'What are you

saying? You, there!' She pointed at Pamie. 'Stop that!'

But Pamie had already hung up with her mom. She dialled Digger's mobile so fast, it was like her fingers were made of lightning.

'Hello?' Pamie, over on the couch, was saying. 'Oh, hi. Helen Regis Whemple told me to call you. Hey, you sound kinda hot. What's *your* name?'

I have no idea how John responded. All I know is, Sheeratikirah, noticing that Pamie was on the phone, had a fit.

'Put that down!' she shrieked. She'd finally let go of me so suddenly that I staggered and had to grab the back of a chair to keep from falling flat on my face. Now Sheeratikirah was streaking towards Pamie, her dagger raised in a murderous rage. '*I'll kill you!*'

'What?' Pamie said into the phone. She leapt lightly and easily out of Sheeratikirah's reach. 'Oh, that's just my friend Lauren. She says she's, like, possessed by the spirit of some high priestess, and she's going to kill us – I think she's had too much Red Bull. Hello? Hello? Oh, hey, Helen – sorry, but he hung up.'

But it was all right. With Pamie having distracted Sheeratikirah/Lauren, enough oxygen was finally flowing back into my brain for me to remember . . .

Dad was convinced there had to be a way for someone who'd been cursed to protect himself, and, sure enough, after months of meticulous tablet reading, he'd come across one: a protection invocation. I'd heard it mentioned so many times (along with the execration texts) at the dinner table, I realised I knew both by heart.

'Evil spirits may not enter a home unless invited!' I shouted at Lauren. 'Sheeratikirah, I command you to leave at once!'

That's when Lauren slumped to the floor in a dead faint. Well, almost dead, anyway.

'My king,' she murmured. 'I've failed you . . .'

Her eyelids fluttered closed.

'Helen,' Pamie said, coming to stand beside me. 'I get that you're new and don't know any better. But no one tells Lauren Woodcrest when to leave.'

I picked up the dagger Lauren had dropped. The tip was red with my blood.

'Maybe you missed it,' I said to Pamie. 'But Lauren wasn't exactly herself tonight.'

'Yeah,' Pamie said, looking down at Lauren. 'I suppose. She *can* be a pain sometimes. My *mom* even says she's bad news. But I wanted to hang with you tonight, so it wasn't like I could ditch her.'

'Right,' I said, sadly. 'The frat guys. Sorry.'

'No,' Pamie said. 'Not even. You just seem . . . kinda cool. I mean, no one else at Milton has the guts to carry a Jansport.'

I was cool?

This had gone from the worst day in my life to the best in a matter of seconds.

True, I'd nearly had my throat cut by the vengeful spirit of an ancient Egyptian high priestess. But another girl had actually said I was cool!

It was at that moment that the front door burst open, and John raced in.

'Helen!' he cried, panting and brandishing a fireman's axe. 'Are you all right?'

'Whoa,' Pamie said, staring appreciatively at John. 'I thought you said you didn't have a boyfriend.'

'Um,' I said. 'I don't.'

John *did* look pretty hot. But then, he always had. Even without the axe.

I pointed at Lauren, whose eyelids were beginning to flutter. 'It's okay,' I said to John. 'I think Sheeratikirah's gone.'

'Where am I?' Lauren murmured. She glanced down and gasped. 'Did I break a fingernail?'

It was clear the protection invocation had worked. Lauren was Lauren again. It looked like she was going to be all right, but we'd know for sure after Pamie's mom, Dr Furst, took her to the hospital where she worked for a thorough medical exam and head X-ray – which she showed up at the apartment to do a few minutes later . . . along with my dad, whom John had called.

'The execration texts,' my dad cried, happily, after giving me a big hug upon finding me in one piece. 'I *knew* they were real!'

'Oh, Lauren,' Dr Furst said, exasperated, when she saw

Pamie and I helping Lauren to the couch. 'What's she done now?'

'Hello,' my dad said, when he saw Pamie's mom, who was pretty hot, for a mom. 'I'm Alexander Whemple. I've just moved here to the city.'

'Oh,' Pamie's mom said, raising a slender eyebrow speculatively. 'Have you, Alexander?'

'My mom's divorced,' Pamie announced very loudly, causing Dr Furst to blush, which was a sight that apparently so enchanted my dad, it caused him to walk distractedly into the coffee table, spilling all the M&Ms.

John had set the axe aside. Still, he couldn't seem to relax. 'Are you all right?' he came up to ask me, anxiously. 'You're covered in blood!'

'It's just a few drops,' I said, laughing. Because it was. Dr Furst had already checked me out and given me a clean bill of health. I wouldn't even need stitches.

'I should never have left you alone,' John said. He looked terrible. Like he'd heard the murderous shrieks of a mummified king's high priestess over the phone. Or worse . . .

Like he'd almost lost someone he really cared about . . . not just got *paid* to care about.

'I can take care of myself,' I said to John. 'I always have.'

'I know, I know,' John said, looking downcast. 'You don't need me . . .'

'I don't *need* you, necessarily,' I said. Then I took a deep breath. If I was brave enough to face down the spirit of an ancient high priestess *and* make a best friend, all in one night, I had to be brave enough just to say it. 'But I do like having you around.'

'I hope that's really true,' he said, brightening, 'because I'm going to be around for a lot longer. Another five or six years, at least. Maybe more. I just got accepted to the PhD program at Columbia . . .'

'Oh,' I said. Perhaps that protection invocation had worked in other ways as well, since I felt the walls of the protective tomb in which I'd kept my heart buried for so long melt away. I allowed myself to love freely at last. 'Have you, John?'

'Yes,' he said. Then a look of happy surprise broke out across this face. 'Wait a minute . . . did you just call me *John*?'

'Yes,' I said, grinning back at him. 'I did.'

Karen McCombie
B.L.D.

'IT'S NOT FAIR!'

That shriek is the reason I *had* to get out of the house this afternoon.

That shriek belongs to Maisie, my three-and-a-half-year-old cousin.

'IT'S NOT FAIR!' she'll yell, the second she's through our door, all because my aunt Nicole has asked her to do something completely unreasonable like take her coat off.

'IT'S NOT FAIR!' she'll scream, when my mum tries to tell her gently that the nine biscuits she's helped herself to are quite enough.

'IT'S NOT FAIR!' she'll howl, when I catch her in my

room, and tell her – through gritted teeth – that pouring my nail varnish on to the carpet is just a *tiny* bit annoying.

I guess it's no big surprise that I've never been able to handle Maisie's whining, but these days it's even harder to listen to. 'Cause instead of pretending to be the patient older cousin, I just want to bend down to her level and roar, 'Hey, you *know* what's not fair, Maisie?! Having your best friend in the world go and DIE on you – *that's* not fair!'

But I wouldn't, because then Maisie would cry (and say it wasn't fair), and later on I'd catch Mum and Aunt Nicole having one of their whispered conversations about me, with Aunt Nicole muttering something like, 'How long's it been since Louise . . . ?'

And those hushed tones always make me want to scream, 'IT'S BEEN SIX MONTHS SINCE LULU DIED, *OKAY*?!'

But if I did *that*, then Aunt Nicole would probably frown sympathetically and say, 'There, there, it's all right to be angry, Sorcha!'

Which of course would make me *more* angry, and I'd want to storm out of the house . . .

Well, I suppose I've avoided all of that this afternoon by escaping *before* my auntie and gremlin cousin even show up.

'Where did you say you were going?' Mum asked twenty minutes ago, as I scrambled around for my mobile and keys.

'Just round to Holly's. That girl from my tap class, remember?' I told her, shoving everything into my bag.

Holly had invited me this morning. She'd come over and

caught me by surprise, just as I was packing my tap shoes away.

Mum didn't ask anything else, but I could tell she was quietly pleased. Potential new buddies for me could only be a good thing – *that's* what she was thinking. Better than spending Saturday afternoons staring at the TV and indulging in my new-ish hobby of biting my nails till there were barely any nails left to bite.

What I *didn't* mention to Mum was the fact that Holly never exactly bothered to talk to me and Lulu B.L.D. (before Lulu died). So I'm about a hundred and ten per cent sure that she only invited me out of pity, or – more likely – some kind of freaky, morbid curiosity.

I check my watch.

Two-sixteen.

Right about now, Mum will be making coffee, and settling down for a catch-up with Aunt Nicole (which will be constantly interrupted by Maisie wailing and wrecking things).

And right about now, it'll be dawning on Holly that I *won't* be turning up to hang out with her this afternoon after all.

That's 'cause I'm standing on the platform at Highgate tube station instead, waiting for a Northern line train to take me to Camden.

Deep breath in . . .

'Warm dust and electricity; *that's* what it is!' Lulu once said, as we tried to figure out what the faint-but-weird smell of the Underground was all about.

Me and Lulu, we *loved* our Saturday afternoons ambling around Camden Market. B.L.D., we'd go at least once a month, heading off straight after our tap class. We'd wander up to the tube station, swinging our bags and giggling about Holly and some of the others and how hard they were trying with this week's outfits. (Who were they trying to impress with their ultra-cool clothes? It was only a crummy but fun tap class in a draughty church hall, for goodness' sake . . .)

But today, for the first time in months, I've just done the same wander to the station – alone.

(The train hurtles out of the tunnel and grinds to halt. Shumf! go the doors.)

'We probably won't be able to afford a flat in Camden,' Lulu once said, her eyes on the Northern line map on the train carriage wall, studying the station stops. 'I reckon Archway's our best bet. It's cheaper, and it's only four stops to Camden from there.'

(Highgate, Archway, Tufnell Park, Kentish Town, Camden Town . . . Schumf! – the door opens to let me out.)

I'm on the endlessly long escalator upwards to the Camden Town ticket office, remembering Lulu's life plan for us both. It was this: kick back for the next three years, then as soon as we were eighteen, everything would start. We'd get university places here in London, our cheap flat in Archway and get ourselves a stall in Camden Market selling funky stuff at the weekends. Although (small detail) we hadn't decided what *sort* of funky stuff we'd be selling yet.

It was the perfect plan.

But then Lulu was the perfect friend.

(Bleep! as the barrier scans my travelcard and thunk! as the turnstile flaps open to let me out.)

I turn right into Camden High Street and my heart lurches when I see the brightly-painted shops spilling their clothes and racks of sunglasses and hats and tat on to the pavements.

The heart-lurch is because it's the first time I've seen it all on my own, and the whole street looks more vivid and busier and scruffier than I remember.

Though I guess the heart-lurch might *also* have something to do with the fact that Mum would *freak* at the idea of me coming here by myself. 'You're only *just* fifteen, Sorcha! I don't mind you going places, but I need to know where you are and that you're with a friend!'

Oops . . . I'm not exactly sticking to her rules today, am I?

'Come on,' Lulu would say, hurrying me along the road, towards the canal, where the Market begins.

We'd swing left, heading over the little cobbled foot-bridge, always glancing at the canal boats moored there and promising ourselves a trip on them sometime, a lazy cruise that would take us past London Zoo, all the way to the white Georgian millionaires' houses down by Little Venice. We never did it, by the way. We always spent every bit of our allowances on amazing finds we'd stumble across at one of the hundreds and hundreds of stalls.

And now here I am, swinging left, walking over the familiar little cobbled footbridge. For a second, I think about chucking a coin in the hat of the busker strumming 'Valerie' by the Zutons on his guitar, but change my mind. ('Don't give him any money – buskers are chancers!' Lulu would say with a laugh, if she could see me now. 'They make a *fortune*. I bet that guy owns one of the houses in Little Venice!')

So I start my meander, winding in and out amongst the crush of tourists and shoppers and gawpers.

How insane is it to think that not a *single* one of them has a clue that Lulu isn't here anymore?

In fact, how insane is it that I can be walking and living and breathing when she's not?

(That was her problem, by the way. *Breathing*, I mean. Particularly that night when her asthma went *mental* out of the blue, and she was gone – *blam!* – practically before her parents had a chance to call the ambulance.)

'Louise Whyte was a wonderful pupil; studious, dedicated and well-respected by her teachers,' Mr Darby, the headteacher, had droned at assembly, once the news had got out.

I tell you, if Lulu had been there, her shoulders would have been shaking with stifled sniggers and she'd have been gripping me hard on my knee, knowing like I did that her mum and dad had only just been told at the last parents' evening that she was on course to *fail* in most subjects if she didn't stop daydreaming and start paying attention.

'She was also a popular girl and a friend to many,' Mr Darby had droned on some more.

Not true.

It's not that Lulu *couldn't* have been popular if she'd wanted to be. The thing was, she didn't care. 'It's just you and me, Sorcha,' she'd say, linking her arm in mine and shooting self-confident, keep-away glares at anyone who tried to swing into our orbit.

Black.

Gold.

Plum.

Turquoise.

Ruby red.

Silver.

The colours of the endless clothes and trinkets and crafts stalls are blurring in front of me as I walk, partly 'cause there are so many of them packed so tightly together, and partly because I don't think I can make sense of the jumble of it all without Lulu here to wow over them with me.

Wasn't it weird that so many people pretended to know her? I think to myself, my gaze idly landing on a board of bizarre small, black rubber *tusk* things that are meant for piercings of some kind. (When we first saw them, me and Lulu couldn't quite imagine what sort of piercings they could be for exactly. Obviously something *ouch*, we reckoned.)

When I say people pretended to know her, I mean *after*

Lulu died. B.L.D., someone like Marina Ashton was just a girl in Lulu's maths class. A.L.D., she's suddenly got some expert insight into my best friend's character, as she told the local paper, when they came sniffing around the school gates. Her quote read, 'I can't believe Louise has gone. Nobody can. She was just this nice, quiet girl in the corner.'

Quiet?! Was Marina *kidding*? Was she muddling up *my* Lulu with *another* Lulu who'd died? *My* Lulu was funny and edgy, with a wicked sense of humour, making shy little me giggle and gasp behind my hands.

Or Ellie Fisher and Georgia Coles, who laid a bunch of flowers by the mini-shrine that sprang up outside the school gates, with the message, *Louise – you were an angel here on earth and will be an angel in heaven.*

Lulu an angel? That's like describing my human-troll hybrid cousin Maisie as a poppet. I guess Ellie and Georgia hadn't ever cottoned on to the fact that Lulu always called them Bert and Ernie behind their backs . . .

Or best of all, Seth Robb, who claimed Lulu had been the love of his life.

Yeah, *right*. They went out three times ('All lousy!' laughed Lulu) and then she dumped him. *Hardly* true romance!

What a joke *all* of them were: inventing lives for Lulu that they could pretend they were part of. How sad was *that*?

Ah . . . there's *another* smell that's stirred something in my battered, tattered brain.

From the alleyways under the railway arches . . . Is it the

Thai food stand? Or Indonesian? Or maybe it's the Cuban one, the Japanese or the Moroccan? Or *all* of them mixed together? 'God, people will try to order *tacos* from me!' Lulu once snorted, holding up the cotton throw scarf she'd just bought from a stall next to a Mexican food stand, and sniffing at the scent of spices clinging to the fabric.

But y'know, even if my taste buds *are* waking up a bit, I don't think I'd be able to swallow. Not today. Not with these multi-coloured, multi-scented memories leaving a lump in my throat.

I need a drink. I've got a bottle of orange juice in my bag, from this morning's tap class. Except it's emp—

Uh-oh.

I've just seen something that's made me stop dead, my stupid empty juice bottle clutched in my hand.

'Are you all right, love?' asks the stall-holder, all concerned.

I guess he gets a few reactions to his jokey wigs – all black and long with that ultra-recognisable bouffant bird's nest.

But I guess he's more used to people straight up laughing, instead of giggling *and* crying, like *I'm* doing right now.

'It's – it's just that it reminds me of someone,' I manage to hiccup, as I root around in my pocket for a tissue.

'Amy Winehouse,' the guy says uncertainly. 'That's whose hair it's supposed to be . . .'

'Yeah, I know,' I sniff, remembering the time Lulu stuck one of those very wigs on her head and belted out 'Rehab' so loud that I half-expected some tourists to chuck her money.

87

'Sorry,' I mutter to the stall-holder, then suddenly find myself zooming back along through the throngs on the pavement as fast as my Keds will carry me.

I bleep through the turnstiles of the tube station ticket office and pad my way at high speed straight down the left-hand side of the endless escalator.

(Screee! The train pulls in as I land on the platform; shumf, shumf! the doors open and close again, swallowing me safely into the carriage.)

And relax . . .

I let my shoulders sink down, as the train lurches away from Camden and my all too fresh and tender memories of Lulu.

It takes me a second or two to realise everyone else in the carriage is hunching their shoulders *up*.

These passengers are the *opposite* of relaxed, and there seem to be two reasons for that, and both of them are illegal.

The busker – the one I saw earlier on the cobbled footbridge – is at the end of the carriage, singing the Kings of Leon's 'Use Somebody'. He's standing up, leaning against a rail, but will wend his way along any minute now, I'm sure, in the hope of someone giving him some money.

By the looks on the other passengers' faces – which read, 'Aren't buskers banned from tube trains?!' – he's as likely to get a fifty pence from anyone here as the *other* illegal, which happens to be a wasp who's currently buzzing itself desperately up against the carriage's plate glass window.

'Wasp! Urgh!' I can practically hear Lulu gasp, and almost

feel her shudder beside me. 'Don't sit down so near it!'

But I haven't much choice, since all the other seats are taken by tense passengers who are pretending to read their papers or fiddling pointlessly with their iPods. As we come into each station, I spy them eyeing the wasp and the busker, hoping one or both of them will get off.

They don't.

(First stop: Kentish Town.)

Y'know, everything about today keeps bringing me around to Lulu, but the song the busker's just moved on to – the Kaiser Chiefs' 'Ruby' – zaps me *right* into her room, the day she downloaded that single. 'Don't you just *love* it?' Lulu said, dancing around her room. 'Yes,' I lied. Why did I do that? Why did I never just tell her that I hated the Kaiser Chiefs?

(Second stop: Tufnell Park.)

The wasp is buzzing a little closer to me, bashing its tiny, stripy body against the glass. If it wanted to make itself useful, it could buzz right out at this stop and go and sting stupid Seth Robb, whose family moved down this way. *That* would serve him right for saying all that ridiculous stuff about Lulu being the love of his life. Though, well . . . I guess it's possible for *her* to be the love of his life, even if *he* wasn't remotely the love of *hers*. And now I come to think of it, was Lulu . . . I mean, was she kind of *mean* to him? I suddenly wonder, remembering the time she blanked Seth in the hall, when he'd come up to her in the corridor at school to say hi. 'He'll get the message,' she'd mumbled to me, stomping away with a little victorious smile on her face.

(Next stop: Archway.)

At the sight of the station name on the platform, I know there's something *else* I've been not allowing myself to think about. It's to do with Lulu's plan for us. The thing is, I never did have the courage to tell her that I didn't want to go to university here in London, or share a flat in Archway. If I get my grades, it's Brighton I want to go to, to do social work. She never knew about my dumb yearning to be by the sea and skim stones into the waves when I'm not studying.

(Fourth stop: Highgate.)

Whoa.

As the train begins to slow down, more strange and traitorous thoughts are suddenly spilling into my head.

It was *me* who wanted to go on the corny canal boats trips to Little Venice, and Lulu who always said no, they were too touristy and corny.

I always fancied trying the Cuban and Indonesian and whatever food stalls, but Lulu would insist we went to KFC instead.

That stuff Marina Ashton said about Lulu being quiet in maths class . . . maybe Lulu *was* less loud, less confident, less cheeky when she wasn't with me.

Maybe that's why she didn't really want either of us to have other friends (she really didn't like it when Ellie Fisher and Georgia Cole once asked me to come to the cinema with them).

That sort of made sense when I think about the girls from tap class. Maybe the others, like Holly, never talked to *us* 'cause we never talked to *them*.

And now it's just occurred to me that maybe Holly invited me round today not out of some freaky morbid fascination, but because she thought it would be nice to get to know me.

Here's the thing, my most traitorous thought of all: my perfect friend maybe wasn't so perfect.

I mean all the *good* stuff – all the reasons Lulu was my best friend – are still true. But then she *could* be a bit controlling, a bit possessive. And definitely intolerant – of other people, of buskers and even of wasps, I guess . . .

Speaking of wasps, I yank my empty juice bottle out of my bag and scoop the frantic buzzing mini-beast into it before it has a chance to realise what's happened (I don't turn around, but I hear someone give a relieved cheer).

Then, instead of going to the nearest door as the train draws into the station, I walk up to the one at the end of the carriage, and shyly chuck a pound coin into the guitar case lying open on the seat next to the busker, the busker who definitely *doesn't* look like he's a secret millionaire with the keys to a mansion in his back pocket.

(*'Thanks!' comes a voice, before the door shumfs closed behind me.*)

As I leap up the escalator, taking two steps at a time, I realise that life B.L.D. was brilliant and fun and colourful.

But I've got to get rid of the grey clouds that have

gathered in my head over the last six months.

There *has* to be life after Lulu.

At the exit of the tube station, I open up the slightly sticky juice bottle, give it a shake and watch as the wasp flits out and off into the never-ending blue sky.

Instead of heading home to Mum, Auntie Nicole and my demon cousin Maisie, I turn towards the bus stop.

If it comes soon, I can be at Holly's in no time at all.

Lisa Clark
How To Be A Star

My sister Nikki is almost exactly one year older than me.

People always say how lucky I am that we're so close in age. They say things like, 'You two must be best friends!' or 'how fun!'

Fun? Hardly.

Let me introduce you to Nikki. She's a girl so pretty and talented and popular that you'd hate her if she wasn't so blimmin' nice, which of course, she is. When I was born, my parents must've wondered what to do with a second daughter, what with the first one being so perfect and all.

Now, I'm not asking you to break out the violins, give me a hug or throw a pity party, because I'm not a charity case. I mean, I do okay. In fact, I'm pretty much an 'okay' kinda girl. I'm 'okay' looking (my eyes are emerald green, which if I do say so myself are rather pretty), I'm an 'okay' dancer and my grades are 'okay', but being Nikki's younger sister at school is tough stuff. I'm constantly in the shadow of my larger-than-life older sibling. She had the entire school fall head-over-kitten-heels in heart with her, so when I showed up, all people saw me as was Nikki Star's-younger-sister-Louise.

Yes, my name is Louise Star, and no, the irony of my lack-of-starshine-ability isn't lost on me.

Rewind to two Mondays ago. On the upside, I scored a seat in the back of PSHE class so I was far enough from the screen to avoid being scarred for life by the DVD on sexually transmitted diseases – icksville. Plus, I shared lunch with my two best gal-pals Aimee and Susie, which is always my favourite thing to do. On the downside however, I auditioned for the school play and all Miss Ricci the drama teacher could say was how completely amazing Nikki was in last year's production of *Romeo and Juliet*. Then, as if that wasn't bad enough, some idiot-shaped boy asked if I got to see Nikki in her underwear – I mean, really? I was getting pretty sick of it all.

So that night, while Aimee, Susie and I were attempting to do our maths homework, Aimee, who was mid-rant about why nobody actually cares about isosceles triangles, stopped and made a concerned-looking face in my direction.

'What's the matter Lou-lou?' she said narrowing her eyes.

'Nothing.' I said, suddenly finding my maths homework really, really interesting.

'Come on, ' Susie sighed. 'We know you too well, Miss Lou, something's up. Spill.'

'Yeah,' said Aimee. 'Out with it.'

'Well . . .' I hesitated, because for some reason it was far too embarrassing to admit that I felt inferior to Nikki, even to my best friends in the whole wide world. But, if I couldn't share it with my best girls, then who could I share with, right?

'I'm so sick of being Nikki's younger, totally less-fabulous sister,' I blurted. 'I just wish people would notice me, for being me, y'know?' Once I started I couldn't stop. I explained what Miss Ricci and the boys at school had said and how it's been that way for basically a whole lot of forever.

Aimee and Susie exchanged glances.

'The truth is, I wouldn't want to be in your place either,' Aimee sympathised.

Oh, now that wasn't the response I was expecting.

'Yeah, as sweet as Nikki is, I'd hate it if she was my older sister!' laughed Susie.

Just hearing my friends say that and knowing they got me, like, truly got me, made me feel so much better, I breathed a sigh of relief.

'Why don't we put together a plan of action?' Aimee suggested.

'What kind of plan?' I asked, a little intrigued.

'A plan, Lou-Lou, that will whisk you out from Nikki's

95

shadow and into your own super-shiny spotlight of fabulousness!'

I high-fived Aimee with a smile on my face, as that was definitely a plan I liked the sound of.

Now, I didn't want to be a giant cliché and embrace the opposite of everything Nikki represented just to establish my own identity, like becoming a circus freak or something really extreme. I realised I had to distinguish myself in some other way. As popular as she was, Nikki was always a good girl: home when she said she would be, didn't fight with our parents, handed in her homework on time – yada, yada. I, on the other hand was more of a wild child, a bit more daring, in fact, if one of those psychological people were to do their psycho-analytical craziness on me, I'm sure they'd say it was because I was seeking attention or something.

'That's it, I've got it!' I declared, jumping to my feet.

'What you got?' Susie asked looking at me with confusion.

'My ticket to stardom, that's what!'

'Ohh, a project!' Squealed Aimee, 'I love a project!'

'Good!' I said, smiling, 'because I'm going to need your help!'

Fast-forward to a week later and it was time to put Project Star Shine into action. Nikki and my parents were visiting colleges and I had the house to myself, so between us, Aimee, Susie and I spread the word around school on Friday afternoon that I was having a party. Not just any party. The party to end all parties. By last class, the buzz had spread and everyone was talking about it. I couldn't wait to throw my first big party.

That night, Aimee and Susie came over early to help me prepare. First, we made a crazy-good party play list filled with tunes by cool bands like The Veronikas and The Redwalls and lots of other bands with 'the' in the titles and gave ourselves DJ names like Miss Behavin' and DJ Spinderella. Then, referring to the throwing-a-party-101 guide we put away all the valuable stuff, like Mum's vase and Dad's golf trophies.

Finally and most importantly, we got dressed. I wore a lacy black dress with a slick of red lipstick and really smoky eyes, Aimee wore a red playsuit with a vintage hairband that Blair Waldolf herself would be proud of, and Susie had on a pretty, pretty black dress covered in a teeny, tiny red cherry motif. If I do say so myself, we looked more than party-ready.

After that, we hung out and waited for people to arrive, which they did. Lots of them. It was better than I could have hoped. The playlist rivalled anything R1 could have put together, people were dancing and laughing and I was really happy. A super hot dude from the year above even added, 'Nice work, Star! Nikki never threw a party like this, awesome!'

Sure, they were still comparing me with my sister, but this time I was coming out ahead. I was officially the Star. Dancing, talking to everyone and having quite possibly the best time I'd ever had.

A few hours later though, and things were undeniably less than great.

A couple of girls got sick and were throwing up on the

bathroom floor – just the thought of how bad it smelt makes me do a little sick in my own mouth - ick. I even found some kids skulking around in my parent's bedroom, despite the beyond-huge sign on the door that clearly said 'Off Limits.'

Panic began to set in as I felt the party slipping out of control, so I gathered my girls who were participating in major flirt action with two boys who I'd never seen before, to help me work out how to make it all better.

'Girls,' I screeched, my voice an entire octave higher than its usual pitch, 'What are we going to do? The house is a mess, and there are people everywhere! This isn't how it was meant to happen.'

'Chill, Lou,' Aimee said. 'Take a deep breath and just announce that your parents will be home in ten minutes so you need them to help you clear up. The house will be empty in five, I guarantee it.'

Aimee was right, the idea of clearing up their own mess was not part of the planned party action, so people soon made their excuses and left. As we cleared up, I thanked Aimee and Susie for helping me to throw an awesome party, because, despite the mess and the sick, it really, really had been.

'Now people will definitely know you!' Aimee laughed. 'Goodbye, Nikki's Little Sister and hello, Party-girl Lou!'

The fam came back Sunday afternoon and, thanks to all my window-opening and air-freshener spraying, no one seemed even the slightest bit suspicious. They were all in a fabulous mood because Nikki chose to go to the same college that Dad went to, which he was not-so-secretly hoping for.

I'd nestled into my bed with a book, feeling more than happy about my new-found party-girl status, when I heard my mum ask my dad if he'd seen her gold earrings.

'You know,' she said, 'the ones you got me for our anniversary, with the diamonds?'

'Did you wear them on the trip? Dad asked.

'No, now that I think about it, I definitely remember leaving them on my dresser…' I heard her say.

Suddenly my stomach dropped. I did a mind scan of the party action and arrived at the image of the kids who had been in my parents' room during the party.

When I'd caught them, they'd made their way out of the room as swiftly as possible. It was them. They'd taken my mum's earrings.

I felt horrible and guilty, and I didn't know what to do. I just lay there, terrified. I tried to imagine asking them to return the jewellery. I was sure they'd deny it, plus I had no cold, hard evidence that it was actually them. At that moment, I realised I was a total fool for having the party. I felt like a huge gigantic idiot for believing everybody would think I was cool, just because I let them come over and mess up our house.

I was disturbed by a knock at the door.

'Can I come in, sis?' Nikki asked, hovering in the doorway.

'Sure' I said, rearranging my face from terrified to pretend-happy.

'I bought you this to say sorry for leaving you behind at the weekend', she said, handing me a T-shirt with a pink-haired character called Lola on the front.

'Thanks, Nikki,' I said, trying to sound as normal as I possibly could.

Nikki told me how much fun the trip was and that one of the cute students giving the tour of the college slipped her his phone number. Of course he did, I mean, why wouldn't he? When she asked about my weekend, I panicked. I didn't know what to do, so I blurted out that I'd thrown a huge party and that some kids probably had taken mum's earrings. I don't know why I said it – all I can think was that it was the good-girl vibes emanating from her that made me confess.

'Lou! You had a party?' she said a little surprised. 'What were you thinking?'

'I know . . . I just wanted . . . I wanted people to get to know me or something.' I said.

She looked at me quizzically.

'I mean,' I explained, 'everyone loves you, Nikki. But people, well, they just overlook me.'

'You're kidding me, right?' she asked. 'Lou, you're amazing! I wish I had your curls, I wish I could make people laugh as easily as you do, and ohmygoodness, you have the prettiest eyes in the entire world – you shouldn't compare yourself to anyone, least of all me, doll!'

I sighed a big sigh. She was right.

'But a party, Lou?' she said, shaking her head.

'All right, Nikki,' I said, trying really hard not to get mad at my sister, 'we can't all be picture-perfect like you.'

'What?' she laughed. 'Me? Perfect? Hardly! I've messed up plenty of times!'

'You have?' I asked, not quite believing what I was hearing.

'Of course! OMG, there was this one time, when I stayed over at Chrissie's, I convinced her to let us light candles to create a spa atmosphere, except I knocked them over, set light to the curtains and a neighbour called the fire brigade!'

'No way!' I gasped. 'Did you get in trouble?'

She came in close and whispered, 'Chrissie and I lied. We said the wind did it. I don't think Chrissie's mum believed us, and she banned me from ever going to the house again!'

I bit my bottom lip in shock that my golden-girl sister had actually messed up. Nikki must have mistaken my shock for fear and she let her arm fall around my shoulder.

'Hey, don't worry, sis, we'll sort this – just give me a minute to think,' she said as she chewed on her fingernails. (Did I mention that Nikki has one really bad habit? It's biting her nails, and she can't stop.)

She was silent for a moment.

'Do you know the names of the people who you think took the earrings?' she asked.

I did. Sarra Pental, Johnny Gaines and Mike Thomas. So I told her and a smile crept across her face.

'Don't worry, sis, I'll take care of this,' she said.

'Really?' I asked. 'How?'

'Let's just say Johnny Gaines has a little crush . . . this shouldn't be too difficult!'

'And you won't tell Mum and Dad?'

She nodded and smiled at me. 'It'll be our secret.'

Now, I love my sister, and I'd never want to doubt her power of persuasion – seriously, I've seen those skills in action, and if there was an Olympic sport in eyelash fluttering and sweet talking, she'd win a gold for sure - but it didn't stop me fretting. What if Johnny denies all knowledge of the earrings? What if he's one of the only boys in the world that doesn't respond to Nikki's charms?

I spent most of the day biting my nails – nasty habit – as I played out every how-to-tell-mum-what-really-happened scenario in my head. Unfortunately, it didn't matter whether I went for the 'I'm sorry, it'll never happen again' route or the 'I just wanted to be liked' angle, the result was the same. I was grounded indefinitely.

I texted Nikki secretly from double Maths asking if she'd been able to speak to Johnny, but I got no reply. Even a manicure at a fancy-schmancy beauty salon wouldn't have rescued my nails from my nerve-induced gnawing, and when I saw Nikki briefly at lunch, sitting with Johnny and his crew, I'm convinced that I absolutely, positively saw her shake her head in a 'Sorry, Lou-lou, you'd better get prepped for a lifetime of bedroom dwelling' kind of way.

I don't know how I made it through until home time, but then when I did, home was the last place I wanted to be. I sent Nikki another text. Maybe if she couldn't get the earrings back, she'd at least be able to help me come up with a plausible story to get Mum not to ground me for, oooh, the rest of my life. No reply. Thanks Nikki, thanks a bunch.

As I walked through the door, I prepared to tell Mum the truth. She wasn't going to like it and I knew that I was about to get to know the four walls of my bedroom in great, great detail. She was sat at the kitchen table, and I slowly slid into a chair at the opposite end.

'Mum,' I began, slightly shakily.

'Yes?' she said, looking up from the paper. 'What's up, love?'

I was about to blurt out the entire I-had-a-party-while-you-were-away story, when Nikki strolled through the kitchen, threw me a wink and put a small trinket box in front of my mum.

'Guess what, Mum?' Nikki said with her eyes wide open in a go-with-me-on-this-one-Lou way.

'What's this?' said Mum, opening the box.

'It's your earrings,' she said with a smile, 'I totally forgot that I'd borrowed them for the certificate presentation the other day. I'm sorry, Mum, I didn't mean to worry you.' She reached down to give mum kiss on the cheek.

Mum pulled a faux scowl at her before she broke into a smile.

'I'm just glad that I haven't lost them!' Mum said, opening the box to see two twinkly little diamonds winking at her in the sunlight. The whole situation was a very typical Nikki thing – sweet and flawlessly executed.

For once, instead of seeing my perfect sib as a threat, I realised that she's my friend. Now, when people tell me how lucky I am to have Nikki as my sister, I agree, because they're absolutely right – she's shown me how to be a star both in name and in person.

Joanna Nadin
A Life Less Ordinary
(Rachel Riley Almost Reinvents Herself)

Monday 13th April

Easter Monday, 9 a.m.

Hurrah. It is now officially week of BIG AUDITION –
i.e. on Friday will be winging way to Hull for two days of
intensive workshopping and character investigation in bid to
secure place on BA (Hons) Drama at first choice university.
In fact, it is now only choice as (a) best friend Scarlet already
has place to do boffiny Politics and Economics there, (b)
second best friend Sad Ed has place at substandard but very
close college to do not-at-all boffiny Music Production and
(c) have been rejected by Manchester and there is no way am
going to Birmingham under Mum's rules pertaining to traffic

systems, architecture and accents. Am not at all nervous as, according to John Major High's ineffectual headmaster Mr Wilmott, my Anne Frank in last year's production was 'like nothing he has ever seen'.

4 p.m.

James (little brother, twelve, self-declared Lord of Google) says *au contraire*, I should be nervous as these days it is mostly about having deprived family background, etc. and I am points down due to John Lewis duvet covers and Duchy Originals biscuits, etc. He says he will be running X-Factor-style bootcamp in dining room tomorrow to put me through my paces as my only hope is to uncover Leona-Lewis-style talent. Tried to argue but he has perfected art of making lips go thin from Mum and is über-menacing.

Tuesday 14th April
9 a.m.

James was suspiciously absent from Shreddies Table this morning. Mum says he has gone to Mad Harry's (best friend of James, also nerd, but with added degree of mentalism). Said he is shirker as he is supposed to be running all-day dining room X-Factor-style bootcamp thing. Mum said he is not as (a) no shoes allowed in dining room following fox poo on sage green shagpile incident (perpetrator still unknown but widely believed to be Dad) and (b) she is commandeering it this morning for internet purposes. Asked what purposes these were. Wish had not. It is horrifying news – i.e. instead of me getting train to Hull on Friday in grown-up manner, she is planning Riley family Yorkshire-based minibreak and they will be dropping me off in Passat and picking me up again on Sunday. Have begged her to change mind, or at least drop me several miles from university but she says she has already Googled crime stats and Hull is rife with murders and mobile phone muggings so she will be walking me to the entrance in an armlock. Is utterly unfair. Will have to pray that all holiday cottages are fully booked or fail to meet strict fixtures and fittings standards (i.e. cotton sheets, Waitrose within ten-mile radius and absolutely no whimsical figurines).

1 p.m.

James is back from Mad Harry's, but he is not alone. He said is no point doing bootcamp half-heartedly so he has secured services of Louis Walsh (Mad Harry) and Cheryl Cole (Wendy Shoebridge – girl nerd, eleven, object of desire of both James and Mad Harry). Said James more like Louis Walsh due to impish aura, to which Mad Harry very much in agreement, but James has pulled his jeans up very high and is refusing to change places. Said was all hypothetical anyway as dining room out of bounds for Mum's minibreak research.

2 p.m.

Is like nun person says in *Sound of Music*, as God opens door, he slams window shut, possibly shattering glass in process – i.e. all cottages utterly booked up due to staycation madness, which was utterly jubilant about, until James took over the Googling and found clean and comfortable eight-berth caravan in Scarborough. Mum not convinced due to excess of whimsical everything and camp shop being not Waitrose but Spar, but James says it will be historical educational visit and they can learn all about 1950s. And then he demanded that Mum vacate area immediately as bootcamp was about to commence. He is utterly Simon Cowell – i.e. demonic and irritating. With helmet hair.

5 p.m.

Bootcamp is over due to judges' failure to agree on anything, plus Louis Walsh tried to snog Cheryl Cole during biscuit break but Dannii Minogue (late addition to panel – i.e. Dog) got overexcited by Rich Teas and did wee on carpet. Mum has cordoned off area while she tackles Minogue urine stain, and also a scuff mark where Simon Cowell tried to demonstrate breakdancing.

Wednesday 15th April

4 p.m.

Caravan minibreak horror has just gone postal – i.e. Grandpa Riley has invited himself, Treena (child bride of Grandpa, from Bolton, wears leggings), and Baby Jesus (Uncle, aged three, addicted to Wotsits) along. Mum uninvited him but Grandpa claimed he is on last legs and could be dead by summer so would be last hurrah and Dad caved in. He is now descaling toilet as punishment. Mum says at least Dog is going into kennels so will be one less mess-maker to worry about.

Thursday 16th April

8 p.m.

Sad Ed and Scarlet have been over for pre-audition talks. Sad Ed said I have nothing to worry about and that I should just be myself. That is easy for him to say. He has notched up a suicide attempt and snogged a lesbian. Scarlet in disagreement though. She says under no circumstances should I be myself and instead I should be her – i.e. semi-emo with TV sexpert mother and adopted sister called Obama. It is so unfair. Life would be so much better if had Angelina Jolie-style foreign sibling.

Friday 17th April

9 a.m.

It is D-Day – i.e. audition and Riley family minibreak. Hurrah! Dad and James have taken Dog to kennels and Mum is making final adjustments to her car seating chart.

10.30 a.m.

Dad and James are back from kennels. But so is Dog. Mrs Peason (formerly overlord of Pink Geranium Sheltered Housing complex, now proprietor of Catmere End Kennels) has refused him a place. Asked why. James said it is because she is dog racist – i.e. she only wants pedigree inmates, despite genetic inbreeding causing behavioural problems and squished faces. Dad said is not dog racism, is down to fact that Dog had bitten a Yorkshire Terrier called Katinka and soiled himself within five minutes of arrival. It has thrown Mum into mess-making/seating arrangement panic. Apparently Grandpa and Jesus do not want to be in the same car. And Jesus and Dog cannot be in same car due to maximising spillage/soiling issues. Plus Dad is refusing to have Jesus in car due to tendency to sing Bob the Builder /Pussycat Dolls endlessly.

12 p.m.

Crisis solved. Grandpa is going with Mum, Dad, James and Dog, and I am going with Treena and Jesus. On down side I have to put up with 'Jai Ho'ing but on plus side we have Wagon Wheels, Um Bongo and Tangfastics. Hurrah! In four hours (allowing for predictable hold-ups on on A1(M), one Marmite sandwich stop and four wee stops) will be delivered by loving step-Grandmother (albeit she is only thirty-one, and lifetime ambition is to be on Jeremy Kyle) on to doorstep of golden spires of university life. Is utterly *Brideshead Revisited*.

10 p.m.

Is not completely *Brideshead* – i.e. golden spires actually more concrete chimneys. Plus halls of residence room is not oak-panelled suite overlooking quad but is magnolia painted box with wood-effect chest of drawers and overlooks car park. But is still utterly inspiring nonetheless. And will not be in halls when here properly anyway, will move into rat-infested student house and live in squalor. Hurrah! Plus have already met potential squat room-mate – i.e. Harriet Jones, who was waving goodbye to immaculate Audi A6 at same time as I was ejected by Treena from the smelly Datsun. She also wearing edgy black vintage despite having tedious parents in beige Marks and Spencer linen. Plus she has completely unmanageable hair. She is totally me!

Although think she may think she is totally *not* me. As is possible may have accidentally given her slightly misleading impression of Riley family circumstances – i.e. due to variety of coinciding events – i.e. floor of Datsun rattling with empty Bacardi Breezer bottles, plus Jesus escaping and me having to chase him round car park while Treena swore at him through fug of Rothman's smoke. Plus when she asked me 'Is that your kid?' did not say 'No' immediately. In fact, did not say anything because could not get word in as she blabbering, 'Oh my God, that is so cool. I wish I was pregnant – it would be utterly *Juno*.' And then we both got excited about *Juno* and started saying forshizz a lot and I forgot about having not told truth about dull reality of Rileys. Is not important. Will make all clear tomorrow. Must sleep now as need to be fresh for workshop in morning. Although am quite buzzy. Is because was late due to woeful undercalculation of wee stops (thirteen, not four, due to excess consumption of Um Bongo) so missed dinner and have had to eat Doritos and Skittles in room.

Saturday 18th April
8 a.m.

Have had possibly only two hours sleep and look like heroin addict. But does not matter. Weekend about talent, not beauty. Am interested only in mind and spirit of fellow auditionees, and they likewise.

9 a.m.

OMG. There is utterly beautiful boy in workshop group. According to Harriet, he is called Milo and is former *actual* drug addict and ex-boyfriend of Lily Allen, or Kate Nash, and has cut on arm which could possibly be cat scratch but also potential self-harm! Hurrah! Also, have not actually revealed Riley reality. In fact, have elaborated slightly on teenage Mum thing. Is not all my fault. Harriet asked about Jesus's father and I said he is much older man (i.e. Grandpa Riley – i.e. not a lie at all) and then she asked if he ever hit me and I said yes (because last week he thwacked me with electric fly swat). So am now potentially embroiled in incestuous relationship with own Grandpa. Which is vile. But utterly groundbreaking. And think Milo is definitely sort to be only interested in groundbreaking girls. Not ones who used to wear days of week pants.

10 a.m.

Think fabricated family thing possibly just a little bit out of hand – i.e. during 'introduction session', Call-Me-Bill, aka Mr Cheesmond, aka head of first year (long hair, knee-length leather boots, no eyelashes) asked us to reveal secret about ourselves. So in Milo-sympathetic mood, I said I had a 'bit of a drugs problem' (did not say had actually thought was herbal headache thing but turned out to be psychedelic mushrooms. Also did not say was one-off and have not done anything else ever unless you count time Sad Ed made me sniff white board marker). But then Harriet said, 'Tell them about the baby' – i.e. Jesus. So did. But also said that woman who dropped me off – i.e. Treena – was my care worker, as my parents had kicked me out (of car, but did not say that bit). Anyway, if you think about it, this weekend is all about acting, and am clearly very convincing actress. So convincing, in fact, workshop piece is going to be based on my life story. Hurrah!

7 p.m.

My life story now also involves a drug overdose, attempted suicide and custody battle. But is all gritty realism, according to Milo. He is playing part of Grandpa Riley, and inspirational care worker who gets stabbed to death by Grandpa Riley (is interesting test of acting skills), hence being replaced by Treena, who is being played by Harriet (complete with random shouty Geordie accent and cross eyes) who is also playing Janet Riley – i.e. Mum (no Geordie accent, but very convincing thin lips).

Milo very sympathetic with my tragedy due to own 'drug hell' story. Is like we are made for each other. OMG. Maybe he is my ONE. Maybe we will snog at after dinner 'mixer' and be utter Kurt Cobain and Courtney Love types, but with less lip surgery and no having sex with Steve Coogan. What was she thinking?

11 p.m.

It is SOOOO unfair. My life is finally riddled with tragedy and it turns out I am *too* tragic. Milo says he thinks it is best if we do not get too close as I may drag him down and compromise his drug-free recovery. He says he is looking for more normal sort of girl – i.e. Harriet. This is utterly typical. Have texted Scarlet for advice but she says it is too late to change tack now and I will have to effect miraculous change of circumstances come September, IF I get a place.

Said there was no need for capitals on IF. Scarlet said yes there is as she has seen my Anne Frank. She is wrong. Will be so convincing tomorrow as myself (version 2.0) that they will give me unconditional place and full grant too.

Sunday 19th April
   9 a.m.

It is performance day. Am in costume already – i.e. regulation drama student black T-shirt and leggings (Kate

Moss sort, not saggy mauve Treena ones), with Baby Jesus in position – i.e. have put Harriet's toy kangaroo Elton (no idea) up T-shirt. Is brilliant. Nothing can go wrong. In just three hours' time will be star of new intake of drama department and potentially get signed up for *Hollyoaks* by talent scout who has wandered in to workshop in hope of spotting next Sienna Miller. Hurrah!

10 p.m.

Hurroo. Have not been spotted by *Hollyoaks* talent scout, am not star of drama department, and instead am back in John Lewis decorated bedroom as Rachel Riley (version 1.0) – i.e. no drug habit, no baby and no tragic care home. Plus reinvention not undergone surreptitiously within confines of Treena's Datsun on A1(M), but on stage in front of Milo, Harriet and Call-Me-Bill Cheesmond. Events unfolded as follows:

9.45 a.m.

Cast and crew assemble backstage for voice exercises and group hug. Rachel Riley gives Milo extra special 'I feel your pain' hug. Milo feels actual pain and has to take two of Call-Me-Bill's prescription painkillers.

9.55 a. m.

Milo still in pain from hug and demands two more painkillers.

10.00 a.m.

Cast assemble onstage. Rachel notes absence of Jesus' father (fake) and suspects potential heroin overdose. Production postponed whilst cast forensically search theatre for body.

10.02 a.m

Body located in sound booth, but is not dead, is asleep. Harriet, aka Mrs Riley, throws bottle of Evian over body. Body does not respond so Mrs Riley (fake) kicks body in genital area. Body swears violently but is suitable revived, though limping. Rachel notes is more in character, given Grandpa Riley's alleged war injury in left knee (not sustained in war, but in ill-advised badminton phase).

10.05 a.m.

Cast reassemble onstage, including limping Grandpa Riley (fake).

10.06 a.m.

Rachel Riley looks up from fake pregnancy test to note presence of limping Grandpa Riley (real) on front row. Also accompanied by full cast of Rileys (real) – i.e. Janet Riley, Colin Riley, James Riley, Treena Nichols-Riley and Baby Jesus Harvey Nichols-Riley (presence later disclosed to be due to catalogue of caravan-related hoo-hah including lack of hot water, abundance of people from Birmingham, and consumption of whimsical décor by Dog). Rachel feels surge of nausea, but decides to channel feeling for convincing morning sickness scene, plus notes that at least Dog Riley absent, so is not all bad. Possibly he is locked safely in Passat. Or potentially has fallen off precarious cliff railway to his death in swirling Scarborough sea.

10.07 a.m.

Dog Riley makes surprise appearance on stage having apparently escaped Passat confinement/railway death. Dog Riley eats Baby Jesus (fake). Mrs Riley (fake) breaks down and has to be given emergency oatcake by James Riley (real).

10.10 a.m.

Production postponed indefinitely due to complete breakdown of boundaries between real and imaginary Rileys.

10.22 a.m.

Call-Me-Bill gets minty and demands that all Rileys, real and fake, decamp to staff room to separate fact from fiction, and also locate wet wipes as Baby Jesus (real) has got Wotsit residue on her vegetarian ballet pumps.

10.30 a.m.

Mrs Riley (real) engages in well-practised Paxman style quickfire questioning. Rachel Riley (all versions) attempts to utilise well-practised avoidance tactics (cough, feign death, blame it on Dog) but Mrs Riley (real) throws in trick question about the mung bean cultivator and Rachel Riley breaks down and admits truth – i.e. that she is not edgy *Juno*-esque teen mother, but is tragically normal product of depressingly unbroken home. And Mrs Riley not evil ex-drunk but sober, if irritating, Marks and Spencer-wearing accountant with Cillit-Bang obsession.

10.35 a.m.

Grandpa Riley (fake) – i.e. Milo – says Rachel should be ashamed of self, and that there is nothing edgy or fun about being pregnant at age of fifteen, or having drunk mother or living in care home. Rachel points out that it is easy for him to say as he is ex drug addict. But on plus side it means she is ideal girl for him as she is completely middle class and dull. Milo says does not know who real Rachel is anymore. Rachel says he wouldn't want to. Milo tells Rachel is about time she took long look in mirror and tried to see who real Rachel was because she might actually like what she saw. Said is unlikely as she has Clegg dark circles inherited from Mum's inbred Cornish relatives, plus hair is mental.

10.40 a.m.

James Riley says whole episode has brought shame to House of Riley. Call-Me-Bill says possibly, but also was very convincing acting. Rachel sees opportunity and says was all on purpose – i.e. utter experiment in guerrilla theatre (not gorilla, know that now). James Riley says no it was not, was typical Rachel trying to pretend she is someone she is not, e.g. Anne Frank. Or Amy Winehouse. Rachel tells James to cease and desist before she tells everyone about time he wore fake furry pants and tried to be Gladiator. James tells Rachel to cease and desist or he will reveal details of time she weed in Pringles tube at Glastonbury. Mrs Riley (real) tells Rachel and James to cease and desist, before exiling them to Passat to think about behaviour.

10.50 a.m.

Harriet comes to Passat to say goodbye. Rachel apologises for possibly misleading details of life. Harriet says she totally understands as her mum has coasters permanently welded to hands to swoop in case anyone tries to put drink down on wooden surface. Rachel asks how Milo is taking it. Harriet says he is reading Sartre in darkened room. Rachel sobs at injustice of it all. Plus because Dog has just jumped on back seat and banged head on her nose.

10.51 a.m.

Rachel takes long last look at drama department, confident in knowledge she will never see it again and will spend college career at University of Stoke on Trent (formerly Stafford Adult Education Unit).

10.52 a.m.

Passat departs for 24 Summerdale Road, Saffron Walden,

stopping only for a Marmite sandwich break, four wee stops (two dog, two James) and one emergency calming down (Dad).

10.30 p.m.

Oh, the shame. It is so unfair. Why was I not born to rock star parents? Then would be drinking vodka with them in Hawley Arms, instead of being shut in room with penitent's supper of cheese and crackers (no butter).

10.35 p. m.

Or maybe Milo is right. Maybe should take long hard look in mirror and will like what I see. Yes, will be revelation. Will see real Rachel beneath shroud of invention.

10.40 p.m.

Except real Rachel still has Clegg dark circles and hair is unfeasibly big. Although could be due to polar-bear-friendly low-energy lightbulb. Maybe will sleep on it. Maybe will wake up tomorrow and will love self completely.

10.45 p.m.

Or if not will go and see Sad Ed. His parents are in Aled Jones Fan Club so he is totally worse off than me.

Sarra Manning
Some Girls Are Bigger Than Others

It was meant to be a summer full of boys. The ones who worked at the funfair on the pier, their tans deepening as the weather got hotter and they took off their T-shirts to spin squealing, sunburned kids on the Waltzers. The packs of guys down for the weekend to our dreary little seaside town, who wanted to steal kisses behind the amusement arcade. The boys from school who'd suddenly got taller and fitter and learned how to look at you as if you were the only girl in the world.

Which was why me and Jules had got summer jobs at the ice-cream parlour on the pier. Before my dad walked out, I used to spend two weeks with my parents in Magaluf every August so they could hurl insults at each other in a

Mediterranean setting. But now money was tight and if I had to spend summer at home then I needed to be where the boy action was. And when we turned up the first day in our matching white short shorts, the owner, Big Don, increased our pay to £5.50 an hour and all the sprinkles we could eat.

Yeah, it was going to be the best summer ever. And then three things messed it up completely and utterly. Jules got appendicitis and was rushed to hospital. Her parents were so relieved that she didn't die that they took her off to Fuerteventura to convalesce. And Jules asked Louise to go with her because I'd insisted her stomach pain was trapped wind. Also I look way better in a bikini than Jules.

Then it started to rain and never stopped. The skies were permanently dark and the sea was angry, bubbling as if it belonged in a cauldron. Our only customers were geriatrics making a small vanilla cone last an hour while they waited for the rain to die down to a light drizzle, and I was devastated at the lack of cute boys coming in for a Cornetto.

Then the summer went from sucking to officially sucking like no summer had ever sucked before. Because one morning there was Rosie cowering under the parlour's jaunty awning when I arrived to open up.

'Oh, hi, I'm Rosie,' she whispered so quietly I could barely hear her over the relentless drip drip of the rain.

'Cath,' I said, giving the door a hard shove because it tended to stick. She was looking at me funny because we'd been at junior school together, but Rosie had gone on to the posh girls' school and she was wearing mum jeans and it seemed easier to pretend that I didn't know her.

She was still the same quiet Rosie who crept round the edges. She looked around the ice-cream parlour nervously as if she expected the metal scoops to spring to life and start attacking her. I opened the store cupboard and grabbed a handful of yellow cotton. 'Here, put this on,' I ordered. 'Loo's over there.'

Rosie reached out to catch her regulation *I Scream, You Scream, We All Scream For Ice-cream* T-shirt, and I realised that she had changed. I mean, she was still small and round and her messy, mousy hair still obscured her pink cheeks, but Rosie *had* grown up. Or at least her breasts had. They were *huge*. And when she emerged from the bathroom in the figure-hugging T-shirt, her tits entered the room half an hour before she did. Large breasts were wasted on a girl like Rosie.

'It's a little bit tight,' she bleated forlornly, staring down at her chest in dismay.

'Yeah, sucks to be you.' She'd bogarted all the breastage so no way was she getting any sympathy from me. Then I launched into her orientation. 'It's pretty easy to figure out, apart from when someone wants to build their own sundae,' I said at the end and Rosie nodded and waited at the counter eagerly like we were about to be besieged by hungry customers.

Surprisingly, we settled into a comfortable routine over the next few days. I'd serve if a hot guy came in but the pickings were pretty slim and I always got the mint choc chip and the pistachio mixed up. Rosie had way more patience at dealing with people and when it wasn't raining, she actually volunteered to hand out flyers because she was a loser.

But mostly I sat reading magazines and Rosie sat reading books. Proper books with tiny letters and fugly paintings on the front of girls who looked all swirly and watery.

We didn't talk at all. Until the day the guy who worked on the face-painting booth came in for a sundae. I rushed to serve him because he was under fifty and passably fit, apart from the whole geek chic thing with his hipster specs and Jack Purcells and, OMG, a *cardigan*, but Rosie was already brandishing one of the scoops purposefully.

I watched in amazement as he took the Build Your Own Sundae promotion to scary places that it was never meant to go. The chocolate ice-cream, double chocolate ice-cream, chocolate fudge ice-cream with chocolate sauce and a flake was against all laws of God and WeightWatchers.

'I saw you handing out leaflets this morning,' he remarked to Rosie, who blushed more furiously than usual. Boys probably didn't talk to her that much, except to comment on her mammoth appendages. 'I could take some for the face-painting booth if you wanted.'

Rosie did want. She wanted so badly that she even gave him an extra helping of chocolate sauce.

'Do you fancy him?' I asked when he'd left with his sundae perched precariously in one hand as he shifted the box of leaflets under his other arm.

'I fancy not handing out leaflets in a sudden downpour,' Rosie muttered. Her voice dropped. ''Sides, boys like that don't fancy girls like me.'

'What, dorky boys in cardigans?'

'Whippet-thin, arty boys with a casual insouciance,' Rosie said, which seemed like brainiac speak for dork. It also seemed like we'd used up our allotted word quota for the day.

I soon realised that Rosie really didn't like me. She would never speak to me about anything not ice-cream related. She'd either bury her head in one of her boring books or willingly serve customers without waiting for them to cough pointedly first.

I tried everything. I asked her about music but she only liked whiny emo bands. I asked her about her favourite TV shows but she was a freak who didn't have her own TV. By the time I asked her what her favourite colour was, I was officially desperate, but she just mumbled 'green' as Cardigan Boy walked in.

He stood there trying to catch Rosie's eye but she was steadfastly gazing at the syrup bottles until I gave her a theatrical nudge. 'I don't serve dorks, he's all yours,' I drawled.

If I'd been Rosie, I'd have engaged in some flirty talk involving the word 'vanilla' but Rosie just waited silently until Cardigan Boy decided on a praline and peanut butter combo. She dropped the first scoop on the floor and, because

I'm a saint, I offered to mop it up, while she tried again. Her legs were totally shaking and when I finally straightened up, it was in time to hear him say, 'Nice badge,' as Rosie handed him his change.

The door had barely had time to close behind him, before she burst into tears.

Rosie wouldn't say why she was crying. She just ran into the loo. When she came out, her eyes were pink, like she'd been scrubbing at them with the scratchy toilet tissue that Big Don got from the cash and carry instead of the posh stuff we had at home.

'Are you all right?' I asked, but Rosie just sniffed and picked up her book.

It was much, much later when I'd just locked up and was gazing at the bulging sky and waiting for the first fat drops of rain to start plopping down, that Rosie spoke.

'I thought he was different,' she said, trying to yank the zip of her cagoule over her breasts, 'but he's the same as all the other boys.'

'He *is* different from other boys. He wears a cardigan for God's sake.'

'No, I mean it was just about these, wasn't it?' She gestured at her chest. 'He wasn't looking at my badge at all.'

I looked at her badge, which was hard because her breasts really were attention hoggers. *Reading is sexy*, it proclaimed, which it *so* wasn't but if Cardigan Boy really had been looking at her badge and thought it was cool, then they were, like, kindred spirits or something.

'Maybe he was looking at your badge but your boobs are in the same area so he had to look at them too. They are kinda . . .'

'Big?' Rosie suggested coldly. 'Ginormous, don't get many of them to the pound, could have someone's eye out – whatever you were about to say, don't bother. I've heard it all before.'

'I was going to say gazeworthy,' I snapped because she could just get over herself. Lots of people would pay good money for a pair that weren't even half as impressive. 'How big are you, anyway?' I heard myself asking. 'Like 40DD?'

'Oh, piss off,' Rosie hissed in a very unRosie-like manner and stomped off.

'I was only asking,' I pointed out, following her because I wanted to get off the pier before the heavens unleashed. 'Boys like boobs, deal with it.' Which was precisely why I had a pair of rubber chicken fillets stuffed into my bra cups.

'Well, I like boys who can see beyond my chest to the person underneath,' Rosie muttered. 'If he doesn't like me for my personality then he's not worth it.'

'Do you want to know what your problem is, Rosie?'

'Apart from the way you keep haranguing me with rhetorical questions?' She folded her arms over the offending areas. 'What is my problem, Oh wise one?'

'You think everything is about your breasts; but they wouldn't be so noticeable if you stopped tugging at your clothes and drawing attention to them every five seconds.' Rosie's hair was in her face and I couldn't tell whether my words were having any effect. 'You don't make the best of yourself. You should do something with your hair and stop letting your mum buy your clothes.'

'She doesn't buy my clothes . . .'

'Well, it looks like she does.' I tried to soften my voice because we were getting off topic. 'Look, Rosie, you might read lots of books but they're not teaching you important boy-getting life skills. Twenty-five per cent of your problem is obviously low self-esteem and the other seventy-five percent of your problem will disappear if you let me work on wardrobe, grooming and getting you a bra that actually fits.'

Rosie took the bait at last. 'What's wrong with my bra?'

I came right out with it. 'You have a mono-boob. There's meant to be two of them, not one long sausagey thing hanging there. I'm not a lezza or anything, Rosie, but I'd really love to know what's going on under your clothes.'

I hadn't even finished my sentence before Rosie bolted across the road and only narrowly avoided getting mown down by a bus.

And that was that. If Rosie wanted to spend the rest of her life being a mono-boobed freak, it was nothing to do with me.

But three days later, after Big Don had been in to give us our wages, Rosie sidled up as I stacked my magazines in a neat pile. 'It's late night closing, isn't it? Will you help me buy some new bras?'

Rosie had a long list of acceptable behaviour for our bra-buying expedition. She refused to have her boobs measured. I wasn't allowed in the changing room. The words 'knockers', 'bristols', 'norks' and all other variants were banned and I wasn't to speculate on what her size might be.

I agreed to everything because even walking to the main shopping drag together was a big thing for Rosie. Acceptance was the first step to recovery, blah blah blah. And I almost shed a tear as I saw the light dawn on Rosie's face as I extolled the virtues of under-wire bras and she snatched a handful and hurried to try them on. She was actually figuring out the basic rules of girl stuff before my very eyes.

When Rosie re-appeared, and headed towards the cash register with her hands full of new bras and one greying old one, she was walking very oddly as if her centre of gravity had totally shifted. Maybe it had, because her boobs were no longer one weird roll propped on her chest, but like actual proper breasts. They were still enormous but at least they didn't look like they should have their own national anthem anymore.

'You have curves now,' I told her in amazement after she'd paid. 'You look super fierce.' I expected Rosie to give me another speech about how she only wanted to be judged for her lame personality, but a tiny, pleased smile played around her lips.

'I'm having this major epiphany,' Rosie confessed. 'I always thought it was superficial to care too much about clothes and hair and it was the inner me that counted. But maybe the outer me should look more like the inner me.'

She really needed to come with sub-titles. 'What does the inner you look like?' I asked.

Turned out that Rosie's inner me looked like the girls in the books she read; quirky and mysterious, which I translated as a muted colour palette and lots of v-necks and wrap tops to minimise her mammaries. We trawled through New Look, Primark and H&M and Rosie tried on everything I suggested. I wouldn't say we were becoming friends, though, more like teacher and pupil.

Every day the skies got darker and the rain got more biblical and we'd camp out in one of the booths, so I could impart all the wisdom I'd acquired in my sixteen years.

Rosie took notes and when I was done imparting she made me laugh by inventing this whole other life for Big Don where he ordered girlfriends off the internet. She was dead sarcastic and funny once you got to know her.

There were hardly ever any customers but whenever Cardigan Boy came in, Rosie would hide from view and whisper, 'You serve him, Cath, please.'

But on Thursday when the bell above the door jangled, I'd just given my nails their second coat of The Lady Is A Tramp, so, with a long-suffering sigh, Rosie hauled herself up.

'Hey, I haven't seen you for ages,' he said and she almost tripped over her feet.

Then his eyes widened at new improved Rosie in a black v-neck sweater that fitted properly with a little felt corsage pinned to her shoulder and a pair of jeans that didn't give her a mum bum. And game on, because Cardigan Boy was looking at Rosie in exactly the same way that he'd looked at his Tropical Fruits sundae. Mind you, he'd looked at her like that pre-makeover too.

'I hope this doesn't sound sketchy but I've got something for you,' he said nervously, reaching into the inner depths of his anorak while Rosie looked intrigued but nervous, because Cardigan Boy was coming over all stalkery. 'I saw you reading *Bonjour Tristesse* the other day, then I found this in a charity shop and you've probably already got it, but the cover's really cool.'

He pulled out a mouldy paperback, its pages tinged yellow. Rosie took it and turned it over carefully like it was some holy relic, as I squinted over her shoulder to see the book title: *To Esme, With Love And Squalor.* What*ever*. But Rosie's face lit up and in that split second she was so beautiful that it made me blink rapidly until she went back to looking like she usually did.

'That's so weird, this is on my to-buy list,' she said. 'And I love old editions of books. If I really like the book, it makes me kinda sad that they gave it away. Do you know what I mean?'

Cardigan Boy knew exactly what she meant. 'I have this hardback of *The Collectible Dorothy Parker* from the 1940s that I found in Cancer Research. Why would someone get rid of that?'

It was all very well bonding over books but they still weren't getting the basics sorted. Not unless I did it for them. 'I'm Cath, this is Rosie and you are . . .?'

'David,' Cardigan Boy said. 'Never Dave or Davy or Id.'

And Rosie totally laughed even though it was the lamest joke I'd ever heard. It was adorable in the dorkiest, geekiest way possible.

How was I going to get Rosie and David away from ice-cream and on an actual date? I needed to try to fathom out the geek mindset but, God, that was so hard. Then, on Tuesday, Rosie was banging on about her latest boring book while I was flicking through the local paper and I had such a genius idea that I almost fell headfirst into the strawberry ice-cream that I'd left out on the counter to soften.

When David finally came in, I elbowed Rosie out of the way, so I could get to him first. We went through the usual sundae business while he cast longing glances in Rosie's direction, then I moved in for the kill.

'Hey, have you ever read *The Great Gatsby*?' It was a perfectly natural question for me to ask so there was no need for him to smirk.

'It's one of my favourite books,' he replied and Rosie

opened her mouth to start wordgasming about it too but I rustled the paper warningly.

'You know they made a film of it, right? It's playing at the Rep Cinema tonight.'

'I've always wanted to see it,' David enthused, walking in to the clever trap I'd set and making himself right at home.

'Really?' I smiled sweetly at Rosie whose eyes were promising a little light torture. 'Rosie's dying to see it too but she hasn't got anyone to go with. I refuse to watch any film that wasn't made this century.'

If David paused for longer than five seconds I was going to brain him with a box of Cornettos, but he was already turning to Rosie with a casual smile that I knew masked the fear of rejection. 'You probably already have plans but if you fancy going with me . . . ?' He tailed off and stared down at his Jack Purcells.

Which was just as well because Rosie was doing a good impression of a slack-jawed yokel. 'Um, if you don't mind, I guess that would be, er, like, all right,' she muttered.

'No, I don't mind. If you're sure you don't . . .'

It was like watching some nature show on the Discovery Channel about the mating habits of geeks. Watching two bears clawing each other into bloody shreds would have been less painful. 'Jesus!' I snapped, pushing his sundae at him. 'Come and pick her up after work. Six sharp so you've got time to get the tickets and popcorn before the film starts. Now go away. We might have some other customers in a minute.'

As soon as he was out of the door, Rosie turned on me furiously. 'You're absolutely unbelievable, Cath,' she began, her face flushing. 'You pimped me! He was obviously just being polite because you forced him into . . .'

'You're welcome,' I said when she had to pause for oxygen. 'If I were you, I'd start on your make-up now because you're still crap at applying liquid eyeliner.'

'He paid extra for the superior comfort seats,' Rosie told me the next day, as we shivered behind the counter. It wasn't actually that cold, but the rain was thudding against the window and it felt like we should shiver. 'And then we shared a tub of popcorn and he squeezed my arm during a really sad part of the movie but it wasn't in a lecherous way. It was a very empathetic squeeze.'

'And then what happened?' I prompted, eyes wide.

'We went for a coffee and talked about the movie and Scott Fitzgerald's other books, and loads of things and then he walked me home,' Rosie finished with a smile that was verging on smug.

'And did he kiss you? Like, with tongues?' Hearing about what Rosie had got up to the night before was the closest I'd come to a snog in weeks.

'Maybe he did, maybe he didn't,' she said coyly. 'But I'm seeing him tonight. We're going to a gig. You should come,' she offered because Rosie was a sweet but totally naïve girl who thought it was polite to invite friends along on dates.

'Nah, you're okay.' I shrugged. 'The music you like hurts when you listen to it.'

'Some of David's friends are going to be there.' Rosie's face squinched up. 'Maybe they won't like me. They're all at university and art college and they'll think that I'm fat . . .'

'You are not fat,' I interrupted angrily because at least she didn't go straight up and down like me. 'You're curvy. Big diff. And you're really smart and funny and you should stop judging yourself on what you think you look like. It's pathetic. And don't you forget it.'

Rosie didn't forget it. Maybe that's why she was a such big hit with David's friends. She even went bowling with them later in the week, then turned up for work in this old-fashioned dress that hugged her curves like she'd just stepped down from one of those 1950s pin-up girl pictures. Her boobs were still mighty but it was like she'd grown into them.

'David's friend Kara gave me this,' she said twirling so I could see how the circle skirt foofed out. 'She said I had the perfect figure for vintage clothes.'

I was happy for her. Really I was. That's why I folded my arms and pouted. 'You could get something in H&M that's practically identical,' I noted savagely. 'And no one would have died in it.'

Rosie's face fell and I felt like a bitch for raining all over her vintage parade, but I could tell she was leaving me behind and there wasn't a thing I could do about it.

We still hung out at work but it wasn't the same. Rosie was kicking it freestyle these days and now I had nothing left to teach her, there wasn't really a lot to talk about.

So it was a huge relief when it stopped raining and the sun came out. Big Don dragged the Mr Whippy machine outside to take advantage of the daytrippers and I volunteered to man it. I couldn't quite master the necessary twirling action but I really needed to start on my tan and scope out the talent.

The sunshine had made the boys emerge from wherever they'd been hiding and I remembered what summer was meant to be about. I'd lost too much time for sticky kisses and holding hands with out-of-towners. I needed to think about who'd still be around in September when everyone at school was bragging about Pedro the cabana boy and François the deckchair salesman. If I had a boy in the bank, so to speak, rather than living off memories, then I wouldn't need any sympathetic looks because newly one-parent families couldn't afford luxuries like package holidays to Corfu.

First, I considered Jimmy from the Waltzers, because he was really fit but he had dirty fingernails and everyone knew he'd done really gross stuff with a girl from the doughnut stall under the pier. Loz from the Ghost Train always winked at me when he came to beg for change but he had a zitty back and he spent off-season in a spliff haze. I needed a boy who was way more thrusting and dynamic.

Eventually, I settled on Kieran from the bumper cars because he played football for the local club's youth team, drove a black Jeep, and when he sauntered bare-chested along the pier with a cocky smile, his muscles rippled and it was like having a religious vision. He was perfect for me.

I pulled out every single weapon in my arsenal. I went two shades lighter on the blond scale, fashioned my T-shirt into a bandeau to show more skin and smiled flirtatiously every time he walked past. Nothing seemed to work and the skanks from the café opposite had set up a tea stall outside the front door and weren't above whistling at him. I could have been invisible for all the notice Kieran took of me.

Summer was limping to a halt and I could feel the weight of going back to school already crushing down on me. I needed a Plan B on the boy-front, I thought as I served up 99 after 99. And as soon as I thought it, a voice in my ear roughly enquired, 'You all right, then?'

It was Kieran. I mean, of course it was Kieran, and all of him was twinkling at me: his eyes, his smile, the bleached tips of his spiky hair. I stuck out my chest and fluttered my eyelashes. 'Yeah,' I said, staring at his mouth. 'You all right?'

'You're Cath, right?' Kieran asked and I forgot the impatient queue of customers and the girls from the café trying to kill me with their collective dirty looks. Because Kieran was all there was and his eyes were running up my legs, over my tummy, lingering slightly at the boobs then coming to rest on my mouth as I poked my tongue slightly between my lips like I was deep in thought.

'Yeah,' I said after about five seconds. 'And you're Kieran. Your cousin knows my mate, Jules.'

'So, like, do you want to go to the Pier Summer Party with me on Friday?' I had to stop myself from squealing because we were so *on*. Every summer, the business owners who rented space on the pier held a party for their under-paid, over-worked summer staff. It was at some cheesy club in town but it was just about the most exciting event of the season. And Kieran wanted to walk in with me in full view of those jealous cows from the café who'd taken to shouting rude remarks at me in their quiet periods. Result!

'Sure, that sounds cool,' I said casually as Kieran asked for my number. And it was that easy to get the guy you fancied – if you weren't Rosie.

I was in torment most of Friday as I tried to dish up ice-cream and beautify myself. There was a hairy moment when I spilled a glob of body shimmer in the chocolate chip but I smooshed it around with a scoop and I don't think anyone noticed. Well, only Rosie and she didn't count.

Once we'd finally closed and I was carefully applying glittery eye-shadow, I saw her mardy reflection in my compact. 'Rosie, you are going to this party, right?' I asked suddenly because I hadn't thought to check.

'Why would I willingly spend time in a room full of

people I'd normally cross the road to avoid?' Rosie said, though a simple 'no' would have done. 'It's not my scene.'

'But you have to come!' I yelped, closing my compact with a snap and fiddling with the neckline of my dress so it didn't dip down low enough to reveal my darkest secrets. 'Is David going?'

'It's not his scene either,' Rosie sniffed, like they were too good to get down and dance to songs that had an actual tune. 'Anyway, you're going with Kieran, so what's the problem?'

How could Rosie not know this stuff? 'Because I don't want him to think I'm some friendless loser who's going to spend the entire night clinging to him,' I all but wailed. 'Look, just come for a couple of hours.'

'I can't,' Rosie said firmly. I'd preferred her when she'd been a total pushover and had no social life to interfere with my plans. 'We're going to see a band and we have to catch a train and . . .'

'God, I can't believe you're one of those girls who dumps your mates as soon as you get a boyfriend,' I burst out. 'You wouldn't even have hooked up with him if it hadn't been for me.'

'That's not fair,' Rosie protested, her voice throbbing like she was getting teary. But she was still picking up her bag like she intended to abandon me. 'That's a really unkind thing to say, Cath.'

I was about to say a lot more really unkind things when there was a tap on the window and I whirled around to see

Kieran raise a hand and shoot me one of those wolfish smiles, which made my knees shake. 'Oh, why don't you just go home and read one of your mouldy books,' I hissed. 'That's the closest you'll ever come to having a life.'

'I can't believe that I actually thought you were my friend,' Rosie choked as she hurried to the door and almost knocked Kieran off his feet. And he could take his eyes off her tits too.

'We were never friends,' I stated clearly. 'I just felt sorry for you.' And before Rosie could put a complete damper on the evening, and to get Kieran's attention away from her scene-stealing mammaries, I dragged him down for a long, tonguey kiss until she was just a fat, round blob in the distance.

When I walked into the party with Kieran, everyone turned to look at us like we were this golden couple or something. I kept a tight hold of Kieran's hand and maybe it was that and the kiss we'd had before that made him so, like, demonstrative.

'You're so hot, Cath,' he kept saying, while rubbing his hand against whatever part of my body was nearest. 'You're the fittest girl here.'

Technically I wasn't, because Lizzie who worked on the rock stall had got through to the semi-finals of a TV modelling competition, but whatever. Kieran was totally acting like we were officially dating and kept the Barcardi Breezers coming. He only let me leave his side to go to the loos where I adjusted the fillets and applied more body shimmer to give me the illusion of cleavage. When I got back to the bar, Kieran was hemmed in on all sides by those cows from the café. I staggered over so I could simultaneously wrap myself around Kieran and shoot death stares at them.

The party was winding down by then, and Kieran and I ended up on a sofa at the back of the upstairs bar. Normally I don't like getting off with someone in public but it was dark and there wasn't much to see; just Kieran sprawled out on top of me while he tried to hump my leg. It reminded me of the fight between my mum and dad when she'd taken the dog to the vets to have his balls chopped off. The dog, not my dad. And I was so busy thinking about castration and poor old Muttley that I wasn't paying any attention to where Kieran's hands were going, which was straight into my bra cups.

'What the hell is that?' he muttered in my ear and before I could process the full horror of the moment, he'd yanked out one of my rubber fillets and was staring at it in bemusement.

'S'nothing!'

I tried to make a grab for it but Kieran was already jack-knifing off the sofa so he could look down and see one breast all perky and firm while on the other side there was nothing but gaping material and he laughed. He actually laughed. 'Are you really a girl, Cath, or are you just a bloke in a dress?'

'Give it back!' I squealed, trying to make a lunge for him but he took a hasty step back and I fell off the sofa and landed in a heap on the floor. Which would have been Kieran's cue to apologise, scoop me up in his arms and kiss me better.

He didn't. Kieran just gave the chicken fillet a tentative prod and sniggered again. 'I heard you were tight and now I know why.'

Okay, Kieran wasn't the most sensitive specimen that boykind had to offer but I've always had a weakness for the rugged bad boys. So I should have known what would happen as Kieran's pack of bumper car mates tripped up the stairs. 'Look what Cath was packing under her dress,' he shouted, as he threw the fillet at them.

I cried the whole way home. And then my Mum wanted to know what had happened and when I told her she said that all men were bastards, then *she* started to cry, which made me cry even harder. Then I cried because I'd ripped my new Zara dress and I missed my dad and there was no one to say that it would be all right because nothing was going to be all right ever again. Not until I got my new boobs and I met some rich guy who'd take me away from this stinking town and everyone in it and I never had to come back.

In fact, I spent most of the night crying – when I wasn't throwing up – and the next morning I really wanted to call in sick. But I had a new appreciation for my £5.50 an hour and the bigger boobs it would buy me so I put on my fake Gucci shades and my longest skirt, which just skimmed my knees, and staggered to work.

Rosie was already waiting for me to open up and I just couldn't deal with her right then. Especially as the first words out of her mouth were, 'You were vile last night.'

'Don't talk to me,' I spat, and tried to ignore the way her face sort of collapsed in on itself. It was raining again, which suited me just fine because sunny skies would have made my head hurt even worse as I sat at the counter and ignored Rosie. By some sheer feat of inner strength that I didn't know I possessed, I managed not to cry for a few hours. Not even when some cow started moaning about the chocolate chip ice-cream tasting funny. I scooped and assembled cones and asked people if they wanted 'sprinkles or sauce?' in a drone-like voice.

I just needed to last until six and then I could go home and go to bed and cry a bit more but time had slowed down to a crawl and there were still two hours until I could herd the last ice-cream guzzlers out of the shop. I stared at the clock on my phone, then gave a little start as it beeped. Then I gave an even bigger start when I saw that I had a text from Kieran.

It was a bit late to apologise but *at least* he was apologising. That was something. I eagerly opened the message and then I really did burst into tears and six o'clock be damned. Once I started crying, I couldn't stop and was only dimly aware of someone guiding me into the storeroom where they sat me down and tried to dab at my face with a damp tissue.

It took a long while for the sobs to die down to hiccups and Rosie was still crouched down in front of me with a concerned expression on her face.

'What about the shop?' I spluttered.

143

Rosie shrugged carelessly. 'I put the *Back in five minutes* sign up on the door about half an hour ago,' she said breezily, as if Big Don's profit margins weren't her problem. 'Is this about Kieran? What's he done?'

I tried to explain what had happened, but every time I opened my mouth, a fresh volley of sobs emerged. In the end, I handed over my phone so she could see the photo of my rubber fillet stuck to a wall and the text: *Feel like chicken tonight? Call Cath on 077557 . . .*

She gave a little gasp, stared fleetingly at my chest, which was as flat as my mood and then narrowed her eyes. 'I knew he was no good,' Rosie announced. 'You can't trust a boy who bleaches his hair. It shows a lack of character.'

It was such a Rosie thing to say that I actually smiled. Until I looked at my phone and my face crumpled again. 'I bet he's sent it to everyone in his address book and they'll have sent it to everyone in their address book.' I hunched over as the enormity of the situation dawned on me. 'I'm going to be a flat-chested freak of a laughing stock. Oh God, it will be all round school too. This must be how Paris Hilton felt when her sex tape got leaked.'

There was nothing else to say so I decided to start crying again.

She totally didn't have to, but Rosie was really cool about it. She let me skulk in the storeroom so I could come up with a convincing argument to persuade my Mum to get a bank loan so I could have my breast enlargement surgery before I went back to school. Then I could pretend that the rubber fillets weren't mine and also start a vicious rumour that Kieran wore a codpiece. It was a long shot, but it might just work.

My musings were interrupted by a knock on the storeroom door, which burst open to reveal Kieran standing there, Rosie's hand round his wrist in a vice-like grip if the ouchy expression on Kieran's face was anything to go by.

'I can take it from here,' she called out and over her shoulder I saw David and a couple of face-painting booth geeks fade into the distance. 'Kieran has something he wants to say to you,' Rosie told me in a sing-song voice and I couldn't understand why Kieran was letting her treat him like a bitch until she did something with her nails and his wrist that made him yelp like the spineless jerk that he really and truly was.

I lifted up my blotchy face and wished that I still had my shades on. 'What could you possibly want to say to me?' I asked dully.

'I'm sorry,' he spat sullenly.

'Why don't we try that once again with more feeling?' Rosie suggested pleasantly. 'Like we discussed after David threw your phone off the end of the pier, or else I'm digging my nails in again and I don't care if it is your throwing arm.'

'I'm sorry that I acted like a Nean ... like a Nean-der ... like a tool last night. It was really disrespectful of me to treat you so objectively and . . .' Kieran faltered and Rosie hissed something in his ear. 'I need to appreciate women for their minds and not just their physical attributes.' He broke off from the script to shoot me a reproachful look. 'I was only having a laugh, Cath. Why are you being so touchy about it?'

'Because you humiliated me in front of all your friends,' I hissed. 'And I bet you sent that text to everyone on the South Coast and now I'm going to have to be home schooled or something.'

Rosie let go of Kieran who rubbed the back of his hand and flushed. 'Actually, I ran out of credit after I sent you that text,' he admitted. 'I didn't send it to no one else, I swear. And I don't mind that you've got no tits, I still fancy you.'

The huge wave of relief swept away everything else in its path. But if there was a footballer in my future who'd lead me by the hand to a world where I was special and important and there was a never-ending supply of designer handbags and spa memberships, it wasn't Kieran. 'Well, I don't fancy you,' I confessed flatly. 'Not any more. Not after what you did.'

He stumbled out after that, mumbling something indistinct though the word 'bitch' was loud and clear and Rosie raised her eyebrows at me and sort of shrugged.

'Thanks,' I said, even though it was really inadequate because she'd just saved my life.

But Rosie seemed to understand because she gathered up

my bag and shades. 'Come on, let's get out of here,' she said decisively. 'You need junk food.'

It wasn't until I was tucking into a huge basket of fries in the nearest pub that Rosie remembered to text David to let him know I wasn't going to top myself or anything. I felt a pang of envy because when would it be my turn to have a devoted boyfriend? 'See, it's stuff like this whole Kieran business which is exactly why I've spent my summer dishing up ice-cream so I can save to get my tits done,' I blurted out before chugging down a whole glass of diet Coke because I was never drinking alcohol again, not even when I was eighteen and legally old enough.

Props to Rosie because she didn't chew me out for letting her rattle on about her own breast issues without ever 'fessing up. 'Maybe it's not your tits that are the problem, maybe it's the guys you go for,' she said mildly.

That was so typical of her! 'I can't help if it I'm genetically programmed to only fancy boys who want the whole package: blond hair, long legs, big boobs.'

'But you said it was all about confidence,' Rosie pointed out – she was starting to sound a little peeved. 'That I should stop worrying about what other people thought of me.'

'Well, maybe I kinda lied,' I admitted. 'Confidence only gets you through the door – doesn't get you into the VIP room though.'

Rosie threw her hands in the air like I was getting on her last nerve. 'You know, if you used your powers for good, not evil, you could totally eradicate world hunger in six months,' Rosie said, as she pinched one of my fries. 'Seriously, Cath, don't you think if you stopped concentrating on making your hair super shiny and chatting up creepy boys, you could use all that determination to do anything you wanted?'

'But all I want is to have super-shiny hair and actual breasts so I can attract a really cute boy with lots of money who'll take me away from this crappy little place,' I said round a mouthful of hot potato. 'Ain't gonna happen any other way.'

'Well, you could study hard, go to university and get a really well paid job,' Rosie suggested but my face scrunched up because I was that close to crying again.

'That would take way too long,' I moaned. 'And I'd make an ace trophy girlfriend . . .'

Rosie's eyebrows shot up so high that I thought she'd need surgery to remove them from her hairline. 'You have to figure out who you really want to be, then make sure the people in your life are going to help you achieve that. Like you helped me see beyond my 36Fs.'

It wasn't that simple but now I was distracted by Rosie's true bra size. 36F? *F?* How could such a thing be possible when I was a 32AA? Before I could ask Rosie, she was digging in her bag and pulling out a notebook and pen. 'You need a proper plan for the future,' she said firmly. 'One that doesn't involve invasive surgery.'

'You sound like my careers advisor, except he thinks my only future is working in a call centre,' I grumbled.

Rosie ignored my whining and held her pen poised over a snowy white page. 'You're very goal orientated, love a challenge and we're going to come up with a project to make the most of that potential. Now, what do you really want to be when you grow up? And if you say "footballer's wife", I'm going to smack you.'

'We'll keep in touch,' Rosie insisted on our last day when we were helping Big Don out by eating our way through the last of the Flakes. 'I'm still going to need tons of fashion advice.'

But we weren't and she wouldn't. Rosie had her own sense of style now and she was doing a gazillion A-levels and had plans to visit David in London. I'd be stuck re-taking the GCSEs I'd spectacularly failed because it was hard to revise when your parents were throwing crockery at each other.

'Yeah, for sure,' I sighed but Rosie didn't even notice my utter lack of conviction because she was dragging out a huge parcel wrapped in brown paper from the back of the storeroom.

'I prepared some audio visual aids for your project,' she said, thrusting it into my hands and smirking when I nearly collapsed under the weight. 'No peeking until you get home.'

When I got home, my mum was well into the first bottle of wine of the evening so I carried the package upstairs and ripped into it. I sifted through the collection of CDs and yellowing books that smelled of damp until I found a note written in Rosie's crabbed scrawl.

Dear Cath

Before I met you, these were the people who showed me that there's a whole big world out there and that who I am isn't who I'm always going to be. I hope they do the same for you.

Love Rosie

It was really sweet of her but I wasn't Rosie. We were completely different people. Like, the huge diff in our breast sizes wasn't a big enough clue. I shoved the package to one side and then Jules called me and I forgot about it.

I kept forgetting about it until one night in October when there was nothing on TV and I'd just dumped another lad from the school football team because he only spoke in grunts. I groped about under the bed and pulled out the first book I could reach: *Madame Bovary* by some bloke called Gustave Flaubert.

I took a deep breath, turned to the first page and began to read.

More great authors to discover
from Piccadilly Press

Tamsyn Murray
My So-called Afterlife

Fifteen-year-old Lucy was murdered six months ago but now she's met Jeremy – the first person who's been able to see or hear her. He may be a seriously uncool geography-teacher type, but with his help, her afterlife begins to look up, especially when she meets other ghosts, including the gorgeous Ryan. However, when Jeremy insists that she helps him track down her killer, she has to confront her greatest fear . . .

'. . . drives along with great gusto, there's plenty of fun to balance the dark side of murder and loss . . . refreshingly different.' *The Bookseller*

Laura Summers
Desperate Measures

Vicky and Rhianna are twins but they couldn't be more different. For their fourteenth birthday, Vicky wants a card from the hottest boy in school. Rhianna, brain-damaged at birth, wants a Furby.

Instead, they get a nasty shock. Their foster parents can't cope and it looks as if Vicky and Rhianna and their younger brother Jamie will have to be split up.

How can they stay together? Desperate times call for desperate measures . . .

Penelope Bush
Alice In Time

Things are at crisis point for fourteen-year-old Alice. Her mum is ruining her life, her dad's getting remarried, and Sasha, the most popular girl in school, hates her guts . . .

Then a bizarre accident happens, and Alice finds herself re-living her life as a seven-year-old through teenage eyes – and discovering some awkward truths. But can she use her new knowledge to change her own future?

Kate le Vann
Two Friends, One Summer

Best friends Samantha and Rachel are spending the holidays with two families in France. As new experiences and boys threaten the trust between them, it looks unlikely that their lifelong friendship can survive this turbulent summer . . .

'All the trademarks of this exciting author – warmth and empathy wrapped up in a story which will tug at the heartstrings of every reader.' *Liverpool Echo*

Hilary Freeman
Lifted

Robyn is a compulsive shoplifter – with a difference. Everything she steals, she donates to charity shops – then blogs about it. She doesn't need to steal, but shoplifting gives her a buzz like no other.

Soon everybody's talking about the mystery blogger. At last Robyn has the fame she craves – but only one person knows who she really is, and he's sworn to secrecy . . . Will Robyn risk revealing her true identity – and can she stop shoplifting before she gets caught?

☆

www.piccadillypress.co.uk

☆ The latest news on forthcoming books

☆ Chapter previews

☆ Author biographies

☆ Fun quizzes

☆ Reader reviews

☆ Competitions and fab prizes

☆ Book features and cool downloads

☆ And much, much more . . .

Log on and check it out!

Piccadilly Press

☆